I0783843

Quinn

FARRADAY COUNTRY ❧ BOOK SEVENTEEN

CHRIS KENISTON

Indie House Publishing

Indie House Publishing

MORE BOOKS
By Chris Keniston

Honeysuckle Texas
Sweet Beginnings
Sweet Surprise
Sweet Temptation
Sweet Deal
Sweet Obsession
Sweet Tomorrows
Sweet Redemption

The Billionaire Barons of Texas
Just One Date
Just One Spark
Just One Dance
Just One Take
Just One Taste
Just One Shot
Just One Chance
Just One Mistake
Just One Family
Just One Rodeo
Just One Surprise
Just One Look

Hart Land
Heather
Lily
Violet
Iris
Hyacinth
Rose
Calytrix
Zinnia

Poppy
Picture Perfect

Farraday Country
Adam
Brooks
Connor
Declan
Ethan
Finn
Grace
Hannah
Ian
Jamison
Keeping Eileen
Loving Chloe
Morgan
Neil
Owen
Paxton
Quinn

Honeymoon Series
Honeymoon for One
Honeymoon for Three
Honeymoon for Four
Honeymoon for Five
Honeymoon for Six
Honeymoon for Seven

Aloha Romance Series:
Aloha Texas
Almost Paradise
Mai Tai Marriage
Dive Into You
Look of Love
Love by Design
Love Walks In
Shell Game
Flirting with Paradise

Surf's Up Flirts:
(Aloha Series Companions)
Shall We Dance
Love on Tap
Head Over Heels
Perfect Match
Just One Kiss
It Had to Be You
Cat's Meow

CHAPTER ONE

The sun beat down mercilessly on the old saloon, its weathered clapboard siding a testament to nearly a century of neglect. Another Texas summer hung over the town of Four Corners, now more commonly known as Sadieville.

Quinn Farraday stood with his boot propped against a pile of broken lath and plaster, surveying the building's skeletal interior with a critical eye. One of the crew carried stacks of broken chairs and rotted tables covered with demolition debris to the front porch. Progress, sure but steady. He liked that.

Returning to the assigned task, his work-gloved hand brushed against the crumbling walls, feeling the decades of history beneath his fingertips. Dust motes danced in the shafts of light streaming through the gaps in the termite riddled siding, soon to be replaced by cement board. Inside, the bare structure would be covered with plenty of insulation and modern sheetrock. He grunted, shifting his weight and adjusting his grip on the pry bar. Another day, another renovation.

Board by board, building by building, Sadieville had slowly been coming back to life. One episode at a time, the dust, cobwebs, and rotted wood in the once-forgotten ghost town, had painstakingly given way to the beginnings of an attractive and inviting small town.

The Mercantile had seen the first transition captured for television, transformed from dusty ghost town seller of wares, to a modern souvenir and gift shop. Next, a nearby group of homestead houses had been rehabbed for the families the town hoped to draw. His brother Neil and his wife Nora moved into the first home. After that came the hotel—and now the old saloon would soon become the local restaurant. Designed to serve the production and construction crews alike for lunch, not that the crews didn't love Molly's gourmet food truck, an air conditioned eating establishment would be a welcome addition. In the evening, this would become a fine dining experience for the hotel guests and growing number of town residents the Tuckers Bluff Council had been working so hard to attract.

The camera crew from *Construction Cousins* reality TV show circled like vultures, their equipment catching every swing of a hammer, every cloud of demolition dust, and of course, every mishap, prank, and moment of shenanigans that ensued.

"This place already looks better." Nodding his approval at the scene, his brother Neil crossed to a makeshift workbench cobbled together from salvaged lumber and unrolled his architectural drawings. "We're keeping as much of the original footprint as possible."

Quinn's gaze flickered briefly to the blueprint, catching the key details. The design would preserve the bones of the old café while bringing it into the modern era.

Tracing a line on the blueprint, Neil tapped his finger on the page. "The idea is to modernize the kitchen."

"Duh," Morgan teased from across the large room.

Rolling his eyes, Neil ignored his older brother. "Open up the dining area. The town council wants something that still feels authentic to the original era, but can actually serve more than lukewarm coffee and day-old pie."

On a ladder by the large window, Morgan laughed, pulling down another small section of lath and plaster. Wooden strips pulled away from the wall, revealing the rough-hewn studs beneath. Chunks of hardened plaster crumbled to the floor, releasing decades of settled dust. "Speaking of pie, I hope they find a real chef. Not some celebrity who thinks wearing a white coat makes them Gordon Ramsay."

"Or some hotshot chef who thinks adding mesquite smoke to everything makes it authentic Texas barbecue."

Ryan, the youngest brother and Quinn's Irish twin, wheeled in a large trash bin to clean up the remaining debris.

Morgan's laugh cut through the ambient noise. "I heard the town council is sorting through over a hundred applications."

"You're kidding?" Ryan's jaw dropped slightly open. "Who knew there were that many people wanting to move to dusty West Texas?"

Neil rolled the papers up again. "There are a lot of people who think moving to a ghost town will be fun."

"Or spooky," Ryan added, his attention falling on the bare wall in front of Quinn. Wooden laths revealed like old ribs of a building holding its breath.

"Or spooky," Neil repeated, tucking the tube of designs under his arm. "I'm going with Connie to look for some fixtures. The kitchen appliances will be top of the line, but in the dining room I need vintage for atmosphere. I'll leave y'all to finish cleaning this place out."

With a nod, Quinn turned his attention to the wall, working methodically, each movement calculated. Baseball had taught him precision—every swing counted, every motion mattered. The muscles in his shoulders remembered the discipline, the quiet intensity he'd always brought to every task.

A particularly stubborn section of plaster resisted. Quinn's jaw clenched. He'd never been one to back down from a challenge. A quick strategic hit and the wall surrendered, showering debris across the floor.

His brothers moved around him, a well-choreographed dance of demolition and preservation. No words needed. They'd been doing this together so long, communication happened in grunts, half-glances, or the subtle shift of a shoulder.

Quinn's hand tightened on the hammer. Another swing. Another piece of history revealed. His focus on the wall, his mind wandering to the next stage; the arrival of the chef. The man's professional know-how would add the final touches of the kitchen. If they continued moving at this pace, the town council had better choose their candidate sooner than later. Much sooner.

The rhythmic tapping of Eloise Carey's knife against the wooden chopping block kept time with the controlled chaos in the kitchen. Steam billowed from stovetops, orders flew back and forth, and the clattering symphony of pots and pans never ceased. Just like yesterday and the day before, this was life in a busy restaurant kitchen. Over the years she'd perfected her knife work—precise, efficient, not a single wasted motion.

One of the waiters came scurrying through the kitchen and shouted, "Table twelve still waiting on entrée."

Eloise's hands moved faster, dicing carrots with machine-like precision. The familiar scents of herbs and roasted garlic wrapped around her, but tonight they didn't bring their usual comfort. Her brother Danny had walked out the door four days ago and hadn't answered his phone since. Ever since being discharged from the military, her brother had struggled to hold down a job, and though he'd never said a word, it was obvious to anyone who knew him how much he hated being dependent on his baby sister?

"Hey." Another waitress paused and frowned. "You're not whistling tonight?"

"Too focused." No point in sharing her personal problems with the entire kitchen.

Hands carrying two baskets of warm garlic bread, the young blonde's brows shot up high on her forehead, but offering nothing more than a shrug, she spun around and shouldered the double doors open.

The last time he'd gone dark like this, she'd worried all night at work until she'd finally found him in the middle of the night, huddled in his closet, hands over his ears, trying to block out the endless city noise. The memory of that event had robbed her of more than one decent night's sleep.

After three tours in Afghanistan, Danny had come home with medals and nightmares. The brother who'd once loved watching fireworks from the Navy Pier now flinched every time an old clunker backfired. The man who so many years ago had taught her to ride a bike, couldn't handle the rushing noise of the L-train past their apartment windows.

"Pickup on seven!" Breaking into her thoughts, a waiter appeared at the pass, plates balanced up his arm.

The kitchen in the upscale corner of the city moved like a well-oiled machine around her, but her mind continued to battle her concern that Danny could be lying in a ditch, shattered and terrified, with the hope that he could also simply be couch surfing with an old buddy, seeking comfort with the familiar. The problem was that Danny needed more than the VA services here could provide. The system was big, overloaded, and in her humble opinion, terribly broken. For years, she'd been at a loss on how to help her brother. But worse, his episodes were getting more instead of less frequent. Coping skills eluded him. His disappearing was happening more often—too often—but this was the first time he'd vanished for so long. Working seventy hours a week, she couldn't afford private therapy, or to move to a different, less cramped apartment. The city tended to press in on him—the constant sirens, the throng of people on Michigan Avenue, the helicopter traffic from three hospitals within earshot of their neighborhood.

"Chef! Need that mirepoix!"

"Coming!" Eloise scraped perfect cubes of carrot, celery, and onion into a waiting container. Her phone vibrated in her chef coat pocket—not the familiar buzz of a text, but the longer rhythm of a call. Danny? Heart pounding, she stripped off her gloves.

Unknown number.

As she stepped into the walk-in cooler for quiet, her throat tightened. "Hello?"

"Ms. Carey? This is Officer Martinez. We're here with your brother…"

Expecting to hear the news she'd been dreading for too long, the officer's words sent waves of panic up her spine. As the calm man explained that Danny was safe in their custody, the nervous edge that had plagued her for days eased. But the news was not all good. Her brother had had an episode in a grocery store clear across town. What the heck he was doing there, or where had he been the last four days, she had no idea. Just like that night, only weeks ago when he'd ended up in the ER, after the fluorescent lights, the crowds, the dropping of a glass jar, the sensory overload had overwhelmed him.

Eloise's hand found the folded paper in her other pocket—wrinkled now from countless readings. The job listing seemed to glow in the cooler's harsh light: *Executive Chef needed for new restaurant development. Historic renovation project in former ghost town of Sadieville, Texas. Rural setting, creative control, housing provided.*

She'd laughed the first time she'd seen it. West Texas? A ghost town? But something made her save the listing. She thought of the photos she'd looked up. The endless horizon. Stars visible at night, unlike Chicago's light-polluted skies. A town small enough that everyone knew everyone. Whether that was a good or bad thing she had yet to decide—still, what it did mean was no anonymous crowds to navigate. No skyscrapers blocking the sun. No constant crush of humanity pressing in from all sides. A chance for Danny to have some semblance of peace.

The listing had mentioned a historic renovation, bringing life back to forgotten places. Maybe that's what Danny needed—what they both needed. A chance to rebuild something broken, to find peace in wide open spaces where the only sounds at night would be crickets and desert wind.

"Chef?" Someone pushed open the cooler door. "Eight top just sat."

"I'll be right there." Tucking the listing back into her pocket, Eloise straightened. Her mind wasn't on the dinner service ahead. Instead, she saw endless Texas sky, a small town waiting to be reborn, and couldn't help but wonder if maybe—just maybe—the crazy want ad that she hadn't been able to bring herself to throw away wasn't some big joke, but actually a chance to save her brother.

With every passing moment, the crazy idea seemed to bloom into an answer to a prayer. By the time they'd served their last dessert and began cleaning up the kitchen for the night, she was absolutely sure it was time to update her resume and trade Chicago's concrete canyons for Texas stars. Then all she'd have to do was convince her brother that she hadn't lost her ever-loving mind.

CHAPTER TWO

Surveying the restaurant's interior, Quinn wiped sweat from his forehead. The new windows caught the morning light, illuminating freshly painted walls and restored wooden beams. The kitchen equipment was due next week—top-of-the-line ovens, cook tops, freezers, prep stations, the works. All chosen with the approval of the new chef.

The Tuckers Bluff city council had finally narrowed the candidates down to two before picking the winner over a week ago. And not soon enough if you were to ask him. Quinn would have preferred having the kitchen fully functional by now, but that wouldn't happen until all the appliances arrived.

Morgan's voice carried from outside. "Sisters incoming."

Quinn looked through the window to see Sister and Sissy heading their way, their shadows stretching across Main Street. He almost chuckled. One as wide as tall and the other looked more like a tree stretching across the street. From the day he hit West Texas, the two siblings, owners of the Sisters boutique in Tucker's Bluff and the former bordello, now a bed and breakfast in Sadieville, never ceased to surprise him. The scent of Molly's food truck wafted through the open door—whoever ran the new restaurant was going to have stiff competition from Molly.

"Quinnnnn!" Sister's 50s style beehive blonde hairdo, as big and wide as she was, preceded her through the doorway. "Tell me the council shared more about the new chef to y'all."

Sissy, the other sibling, sported red hair and stood

almost a head taller than her sister and rail-thin to boot. The two ducked under a ladder where Ryan was touching up trim. "Frankly, I don't understand what the big secret is. Unless they've hired Gordon Ramsey—"

"Lord forbid," her sister cut her off.

Sissy rolled her eyes at her sister. "Honestly, what do they think keeping the head chef's name and details a secret will do?"

Considering these two women as well as his aunt Eileen and the rest of the Tuckers Bluff Afternoon Social Club were usually the first to know anything and everything about everyone in town, not knowing this must be killing them. All Quinn could do was shrug.

"Well," Sister huffed, "at least we have the B&B all spruced up. We want Sadieville to make a good impression. We've put him in the Violet Room—best view of the sunrise." She rocked on the balls of her feet and sighed. "So, they didn't tell you anything more about him at all?"

Quinn checked his watch. The crew would be breaking for lunch about now, but he suspected he wouldn't be going anywhere until the sisters got some answers. Too bad he didn't have what they wanted. "All I know is that the chef's due in three days. And before you ask, no, I don't know anything else except he's from Chicago."

"Chicago!" Sister clutched her chest. "Oh, I do hope he likes our sleepy little town."

"Now now, Sister, don't get your pearls in a cluster. I'm sure the town wouldn't have chosen a big city chef if they didn't have good reason for wanting to live in dusty West Texas."

"I sure hope you're right." Sister spun around to face Quinn and his brothers. "We're supposed to meet your aunt Eileen for lunch, but she called to say Connor needed her to baby-sit last minute. You boys taking a break for lunch?"

Morgan stepped to the fore front. "Yes, ma'am."

Grabbing his hat from the hook by the door, Quinn slapped it against his thigh and nodded. The production crew had stopped filming as soon as the sisters came to the door. Now most of the crew was halfway across the street, the smell of whatever Molly was cooking up calling to everyone like a siren's song.

At the truck, Molly looked up from the window, a lock of curly hair escaping its bandana. "What can I get you boys today?"

To his delight, Molly's famous brisket tacos and fried mac and cheese were on the menu. "My usual."

Molly smiled at him. "Better give you your fill. Once the restaurant opens, you may not be so hungry."

"Now Molly," Sister patted her hand, "you know your food truck is an institution. Not everyone wants a sit-down restaurant."

"Besides," Sissy added, "different clientele entirely. You feed these hardworking men their lunch." She winked at Quinn. "The restaurant will be for tourists who want to pretend they're dining in the Old West."

Quinn accepted his lunch from Molly. Ever since her heart attack not too long ago, folks in town had been worried she worked too hard. Staying open late, some nights really late, so that the crews could eat when filming ran long had to be hard on her. He thought that maybe that was one of the reasons the town council and the production company agreed to move the restaurant up, instead of doing the spa or another building on Main Street.

Savoring their lunch, there was plenty of oohs, aahs, yums, and finger licking.

"I hope whoever the new chef is that the menu is as good as Molly's." Morgan wiped his mouth. "Because if it is, this town's going to be inundated with tourists."

"And townsfolk from Tuckers Bluff," Sister added, her expression turning contrite, facing the brothers. "Not that the Farraday pub and town café in Tuckers Bluff aren't good places to eat, but you know what they say about variety—."

Her sister cut her off, finishing her sentence. "It's the spice of life."

Excusing himself from the picnic table they'd all been seated at, Quinn headed back to work, catching fragments of conversation floating on the breeze—speculation about the new chef, plans for welcome baskets, debates about proper Texas hospitality. He had no idea what all the fuss was about. The new chef was arriving shortly, the appliances would be installed soon after, and then the restaurant would open. What was the big deal?

"Did you get the new appointment schedule?" Eloise pressed her phone closer to her ear, trying to hear Danny over the airport announcements.

"Third time you've asked, Sis." His voice was steady—a good sign. "Three more weeks of therapy, then Dr. Marshall will authorize the transfer of my care to the VA clinic in Midland. She says it's actually got a great PTSD program."

If only he hadn't had that last episode, the VA might have approved him to transfer in time to leave with her. Eloise watched a young family struggle past with too much luggage. "And you'll be okay in the apartment alone? Mrs. Kowalski next door said—"

"El." Danny's tone held the echo of the big brother he used to be. "I've got this. The city's not going to break me. Not with an end date in sight." A pause. "Besides, if you want your deposit back, that crusty old landlady likes me better than you."

She smiled despite the knot in her stomach. "Maybe, but remember…"

"I know. Three more weeks. The movers will come and pack up what's left of the place. One night at the airport hotel, a flight to Midland, check in with the VA, then we'll settle down in Hooterville."

Again, it was so nice to hear her brother's teasing sense of humor referring to that ancient retro TV show. "Sadieville."

The gate agent's voice cut through their conversation: "Now boarding Group two for flight 2247 to Midland, Texas."

"That's me." Eloise gripped her carry-on. "I'll call you when I land."

"Hey El?" Danny's voice softened. "Thanks. For finding us somewhere… quieter."

Tears pricked at her eyes. "Love you, big brother."

"Love you too, chef."

Eloise tucked her phone away, joining the boarding line. Each step felt surreal, like she was walking into someone else's life. Chicago's morning rush hour was just ramping up outside the airport windows—horns honking, trains rumbling, the city awakening to its daily chaos. In a few hours, she'd be in Texas, where the only traffic might be the whispering sounds of tumbleweeds rolling through town. Lord she hoped it wasn't really that bad. After all, she understood this was just the beginnings of a new tourist community, but hopefully it would be everything her brother needed.

The flight attendant scanned her boarding pass. "Seat 12A, on your left."

Window seat. Perfect. Eloise stowed her bag and settled in, her mind already racing ahead. The production company's car would meet her at Midland Airport. Then she'd be taken to her new home. In Sadieville. A ghost town. She didn't know whether to laugh or take her temperature. She was moving to a literal ghost town.

The plane backed away from the gate, and Chicago's skyline filled her window. Somewhere down there, Danny was probably doing his breathing exercises, focusing on the techniques that helped him cope with the urban assault on his senses. Three weeks. They just had to get through three more weeks apart.

The plane turned toward Texas, and Eloise closed her eyes. She'd packed her favorite knives in her checked bags, precious pieces of her Chicago life hand-washed, wrapped in cloth then bubble wrap and insured for as much as she was allowed. Doing her best to relax, not worry, embrace the change, her mind wandered to the first episode of *Construction Cousins*. Curious while waiting for her next interview with the Tuckers Bluff town council, she streamed the available episodes.

Impressed with the camaraderie between the brothers, their skill, and their craftsmanship, she found herself continually distracted by deep southern voices that settled over her as smoothly as a napoleon brandy. And then there was the jeans. Lord did those brothers know how to wear a pair of pants. Thank heaven she wasn't going to be working up close and personal with any of the brothers, she'd lose all her fingers chopping her vegetables and trying not to watch them. She didn't care whether or not she was caught on film, as long as it wasn't eyeing the hunky hammer wielding cowboys. Yep, she had one mission, save her brother and stay away from the smooth-talking Construction Cousins.

Easy peasy.

The next thing she knew, the sound of the captain's voice over the loudspeaker announcing their approach to the Midland-Odessa airport drew her out of a deep sleep. Maybe this was a good sign that for the first time in months, she was finally able to get some decent sleep, even in the uncomfortable seat of an airplane.

Her carryon flung over her shoulder, she exited the plane and followed the trail of passengers like ants to a picnic. By the carousel, her name sprawled across a cardboard sign caught her eye. Next phase of her journey had gone off without a hitch, she wasn't stranded at the airport in the middle of nowhere. She would happily take this as a sign that she'd made the right choice.

In no time at all, her bags were in the trunk of the car and she was driving through oil country Texas to her new home. Just as she'd done on the plane, after miles of West Texas dirt, she'd grown bored with the scenery and fallen asleep. Not till the car bounced over uneven ground did she open her eyes. Ahead she could see the small town in the distance. It didn't look like much, but it was blissfully quiet.

The car drove over a slight hump and the rest of the way to town was smooth concrete. She couldn't help but wonder if road repair was on the to-do list for the Construction Cousins. In minutes, the sleek black SUV pulled up in front of a beautifully restored old building with white-washed shipboard, crisply painted shutters, and colorful pots painted with fresh flowers. To her surprise, the driver carried her bags down the front walkway. This was too large a house just for her. Maybe there was an upstairs apartment, or a guest house in the backyard.

No sooner had she stepped onto the curb than two women came scurrying out. "Welcome to the Parlor B&B."

A little confused, Eloise muttered, "Hello."

"Do you have a reservation?" the tall redhead asked. "If you don't that's just fine. We have plenty of rooms."

"At least till next week," the shorter blonde woman spoke up. "There's a big group of Red Hat ladies coming to stay."

All she could do was nod and smile. She was good at smiling, even when she had no idea what was going on. "I'm Eloise Carey, the chef for the town's new restaurant."

The two women's brows rose high on their foreheads in precise synchronization before they turned to face each other, shrugged, then turning back sporting identical grins.

"We were expecting a man," the blonde said.

"And aren't you a nice surprise." The redhead slipped her arm inside the crook of Eloise's elbow and began walking.

Back home, Eloise would have gone into panic mode, but here, here she felt like she'd just been whisked away by a favorite grandmother.

"I'm sure you're going to love it here," the redhead continued. "We've given you the best room."

"It has the nicest view." The other woman hurried along at her side.

"Room?" Eloise mumbled. "You must be mistaken. The agreement called for an apartment."

The two women leaned slightly forward, once again looking at each other before straightening and smiling at her.

The redhead must be the leader of the pack, because she spoke first. "I'm sure the misunderstanding will be straightened out soon enough, but for now, we'll take very good care of you."

She didn't let her smile slip, and even though she believed every word the women said, especially about taking care of her, something deep in her gut told her that her good start had just taken a nose dive.

CHAPTER THREE

The warmth of early morning baking lingered in the old brothel turned B&B's kitchen. Humming, Eloise arranged her pastries with precision—croissants golden-brown and flaky, bear claws dusted with powdered sugar, cinnamon rolls with just the right swirl. She'd risen before dawn, grateful Sister and Sissy had welcomed her use of their commercial kitchen. It had been a very long time since she'd woken up and felt like singing. Despite the surprise of finding herself in a B&B and not her own furnished apartment, life was looking good. Very good. After all, she had weeks before Danny's arrival to fix the housing error.

The Sisters had been a whirlwind of hospitality since her arrival. Having grown up in the foster care system, Eloise had always envisioned what it would be like to have a family, and these two ladies with their perkiness and eagerness to indulge her, certainly fit the image she'd created of sweet grandmothers. Not that either of the women were old enough to be her grandmother, but they still fit the bill.

"Oh, my." Sister took a slow moanful bite. "Don't tell Toni I said this, but I think she's got some stiff competition."

"Toni?"

"Yes," Sissy nodded in agreement, her tall frame leaning against the kitchen counter, "Toni's Brook Farraday's wife. The town gained ten pounds a person when she moved to Tuckers Bluff, married Brooks, and began supplying the Silver Spoon Café with fresh baked goods."

"And don't forget Meg's B&B. Her guests get early

morning treats too," Sister mumbled over another bite.

"I swear," Sissy smiled, "watching you work with the precision of a military strategist has been very interesting. I think this is the most use this new kitchen has seen all year."

Carefully, Eloise arranged everything on a professional catering tray. According to the bag Sister had pressed into her hands that morning, the coffee came from a local roaster. The rich, robust aroma of Colombian beans combined with her secret ingredient would hopefully give folks a hint at the culinary expertise she was bringing to Sadieville. The final approval from the city council had given her carte blanche with the restaurant. So many ideas had ricocheted in her mind. She could hardly wait to begin. Even though she would not be the proprietor of this new venture, the body and soul of the restaurant would be all her. The coffee was just a smidge of a prelude.

Although the apartment mix-up still niggled at the back of her mind, making her wonder what else might not be as expected, Sissy's words echoed with reassuring certainty. "Not to worry, dear. Things have a way of working out in our neck of the woods."

Danny would laugh if he could see her now. Her big-city chef persona transplanted into this reviving ghost town, carrying pastries like a white flag. She'd faced tough crowds in Chicago's cutthroat restaurant scene. A bunch of contractors and their television crew would be a piece of cake—so to speak—to win over.

The crisp morning air brightened her already good mood. A delightful change from the icy mornings in Chicago. West Texas dust danced around her feet as she walked toward the restaurant site. Some day, when she had to clean her home, the dusty air might be a problem, but for now she felt like a time traveler walking into the Wild West. Any minute now, she almost expected to see Miss Kitty emerge from the still neglected saloon. How silly was that, but it did confirm one thing, the folks who planned the revival of this old town knew what they were doing.

Construction vehicles lined the street, workers moving

about with purpose. The TV crew was already setting up, cameras positioned to catch every moment of the renovation. This wasn't just a restaurant—it was a performance, and already she could feel the energy crackling in the air around her. This was going to be so much more fun than she'd expected. To think, she and her new restaurant would be a part of the rebirth of a town's history.

Adjusting her grip on the tray, she resisted the urge to brush at her chef whites—crisp, professional, a statement of her capabilities. The fabric was a second skin, a uniform that spoke of years of hard work, of kitchens where only the strongest survived. She was ready to make a good first impression.

A man stood with his back to her, directing workers. Broad shoulders, work boots, the kind of stance that suggested he was used to being in charge. Must be one of the Farraday brothers—the Construction Cousins themselves. She'd watched enough of their show to recognize that particular brand of Texas confidence.

"Excuse me," she called out.

The man turned, and Eloise found herself looking up—way up—at a wall of muscle and stern expression. This was definitely not the welcome she'd imagined. Up close, he was even more imposing. Carved from granite, with deep steel blue eyes that seemed to look right through her.

"Delivery's around back," he muttered, not bothering to look fully her way.

For a moment, her good mood wavered. She'd left behind everything for this moment and this was her welcome? Straightening her spine, lifting her chin, widening her smile, she cleared her throat. "I'm Eloise Carey."

The man barely glanced her way, already turning back to the workers. "Yes. Delivery's still around back."

Not letting her smile slip or her good mood wither, gripping the tray more tightly, she followed him. Her steps quick, her stride determined. "I don't think you understand."

"Of course I do." He glared down at her, handed her a five-dollar bill, and turned away. "Delivery is still around back."

He walked faster.

She walked faster.

The TV cameras were definitely catching this now. Perfect. Absolutely perfect.

Never in his life had Quinn met such a determined delivery person. Not even a healthy tip slowed her down.

"Mister. I. Am. Not. Making. A. Delivery." The sternness in her tone had him stopping mid step. "I'm the new executive chef for the restaurant."

"Oh, good." His sister-in-law, Valerie, the producer of the show, the one with the bright idea that had roped all of them into this crazy reality TV show business, stood grinning at them like the Cheshire Cat. "I see you've met Eloise Carey, our new executive chef."

Quinn stared at the petite woman who didn't look strong enough to carry anything heavier than a cup of coffee, never mind a heavy sauce pan. His mind scrambling to process what the two women had just told him. The new chef was this tiny woman who barely reached his shoulder? This slip of a thing who'd been chasing him around the construction site with pastries? "Chef?"

The woman let out a deep sigh, raised her gaze heavenward, all while continuing to balance the tray of coffee and pastries. "I've been trying to tell you that."

His face heated. He'd dismissed her, handed her a tip, and walked away. Multiple times. And the cameras had caught every second of it. He'd love to think it would make the cutting room floor, but this was exactly the sort of faux pas the production crew loved to capture—and air on television.

"Cut!" the director called out, practically bouncing on her toes. "That was perfect! The viewers are going to love this. The gruff contractor and the determined chef. Pure gold."

His gaze darting to where Valerie stood still grinning like a fool, Quinn shot his sister-in-law a glare that would have wilted a cactus. Somehow she just grinned wider.

"Now," the director continued, "let's get some shots of you showing Chef Carey the kitchen layout. Quinn, you can explain the modifications we made to accommodate the equipment she specified."

Chef Carey's expression brightened. "All of it?"

"Everything exactly as you requested," he managed, still thrown by this turn of events. He'd expected… well, he wasn't sure what he'd expected, but not this woman with her determined stride and professional demeanor who somehow made him feel like he was the one who needed to catch up.

"Perfect." Glancing around, she hesitated, then spinning about, faced Valerie. "I brought this for the crew. Where can I set them down?"

Overhearing her, Ryan came strolling over, his nose sniffing the air like a hound dog on a trail. "Are those still warm?"

Her chest puffed with pride, the new chef nodded. "Fresh out of the oven."

Like moths to a flame, the petite woman was surrounded by most of the crew reaching around, chewing, muttering, and raving about the surprise treat.

With the tray being passed around, and everybody loving the fresh baked goods, the chef rocked on the balls of her feet, and smiled as if she'd been given an Academy Award for cooking. Looking extremely content with herself, and awfully cute to boot, she turned and took a step inside. "If it's okay, I'd love to check the spacing."

At his and Valerie's nod, she strode into the building and quickly pulled a measuring tape from her pocket. Moving through the space with purpose, she checked corners, examined surfaces, nodding to herself at every turn.

"The ventilation system?" she called out.

Quinn took a step closer. "Commercial grade. Top of

the line. Meets both yours and the architect's specifications."

Her sunny grin made her caramel colored eyes sparkle. "Good. The gas lines?"

"Tested yesterday."

Ryan wandered over, chomping away on a massive pastry. "These are amazing."

"Thank you," she called out, not looking up from her measurements. "I'm not really a baker, but I did a brief stint in Paris and learned a few tricks."

Swallowing another bite, Ryan turned to his brother. "Aren't you going to try one?"

Glancing at the last two pastries in the tray someone had set down on a pair of saw horses, he debated between shaking his head on principle and pouncing on the sweet treat before they were all gone.

Still nodding and smiling at the layout of her new kitchen, Eloise called over her shoulder at no one in particular, "Coffee's probably getting cold too."

Gleefully rubbing her hands together, Valerie leaned into both Ryan and Quinn. "I love surprises like this. The human touch. The viewers will eat this up—a woman who knows what she wants and within minutes of her arrival has the whole crew, literally, eating out of her hands. This is going to be our best episode yet."

Quinn watched as Chef Carey paced out the dining room space, muttering calculations under her breath. She moved like someone who knew exactly what she wanted and how to get it. Each step precise, each measurement careful. Somehow, despite the thoughtful glare, she still managed to sport the slightest of smiles.

She spun to face him, those same caramel eyes with specks of gold were bright with intelligence and something that looked suspiciously like amusement.

Morgan appeared at his shoulder, biting into a second— or was it his third—croissant. "If you spoil us like this every day, we're all going to be rolled out of here in a wheel barrow."

Reaching for the last croissant, Valerie took a bite and

moaned. "Oh my, these are as good as Toni's. Maybe better." Immediately, her hand flew to her mouth, her eyes rounded like an insomniac owl. "Oh, dear. Don't tell her I said that."

A wave of chuckles moved through the room, but Morgan was the one to lean over, kiss his wife on the tip of her nose, and with adoring eyes that made Quinn both delighted that after all this time his brother was still so happy, and a bit envious that he had yet to find the love of his life, whispered just loud enough for Quinn to hear, "Your secrets are always safe with me."

Valerie's cheeks flushed with a tinge of dark rose and somehow Quinn suddenly felt like he was invading their privacy.

Measuring tape still in hand, and one side of her mouth tipped higher than the other in a cute little grin, the new chef chuckled softly, the sound warming the updated space. "If you like my pastries, wait until you taste my beef bourguignon. That will make your taste buds really sing."

Did taste buds sing? Quinn snatched the last pastry, took a bite, bit back a delighted moan, and had to wonder, would these have tasted so dang good if Eloise were a man?

CHAPTER FOUR

A beat-up old truck pulled into the front of the soon-to-be new restaurant in town. A woman in worn jeans, a long sleeve checkered shirt, and a tan cowboy hat hopped out of the passenger door, a large gray dog a leap behind her. Hurrying onto the old wooden sidewalk, the woman surveyed the room with a quick glance and smiled at no one in particular. "Sorry I'm late, but Gray here refused to stay home."

Finishing up her inspection of the kitchen and dining room, Eloise got the feeling from the way everyone in the place stopped that this woman was someone important.

"Is he here? Does he like it? What did I miss?"

Ryan chuckled and casting a sideways glance to his brother Morgan, bit back his smile, and raised what was left of his croissant. "Well, the morning baked goods were a hit."

"Oh." The woman's eyes widened. "He bakes too?"

The gray dog heeling at her side perked his ears with interest, his gaze seemed to be studying Eloise. If she didn't know better, she'd swear the dog understood she was the baker and wanted a treat too.

Footsteps pounded against the wooden walkway, slowing as the two women from the B&B raced through the doorway. Hands on their chests, anyone would think they'd run a marathon and not a few yards down Main Street. "Oh, Eileen, you're here. Have they told you about the problem?"

"They? Problem?" The woman's gaze narrowed.

Morgan shook his head. "I don't see why it's a problem."

Hands on their hips, the two women glared at him. "Of

course it's a problem."

Clearing his throat, Quinn took a step closer to the woman with the hat. "I know y'all were expecting a man but I don't see why a woman is a problem."

"Woman?" Eileen's forehead crumpled, showing her confusion. "What woman? What are y'all talking about?"

"Oh, for lands sake," Sister sighed.

"I think he means me." Eloise raised one hand, smiled, and wiggled her fingers at the lady. "I'm Eloise Carey."

Instantly, the woman's frown slipped and a wide smile replaced it as she extended her hand. "Eileen Farraday, pleasure to meet you." Stepping back after shaking hands, Eileen looked at the others. "I still don't know what the heck y'all are talking about."

Sissy pushed past her taller sister and frowned at the two men standing to one side. "Really, you two." Shaking her head at the men, she turned to Eileen and smiling, gestured toward Eloise. "Eloise is our new chef, and these two buffoons think the problem is that she's not a man."

Frowning again, Eileen turned to Quinn and Morgan. "Why in the name of God's country would that be a problem?"

Chuckling under his breath, Ryan held his hands up, palms out, and retreated a couple of steps, shaking his head, while his two brothers coughed and sputtered like an old muffler.

"Speak up," the woman urged.

"Sorry, ma'am." Quinn looked terribly contrite. "It's just that most folks were expecting a man."

"And?" Now Eileen was tapping her booted toe on the floor.

Quinn cleared his throat. "And we're looking forward to her beef bourguignon."

How silly was it that her heart skipped a beat because the man not only heard her brag about her favorite dish, but remembered as well.

"It's the apartment," Sister said. "That blasted city council never told her that the apartment they promised her isn't going to be ready for some time."

"That's right," Sissy nodded. "Poor thing had no idea

she was going to be staying with us at the Parlor House. Not that she minds it, but her brother is coming and we didn't save a room for him."

"Apartment?" Quinn turned to Sissy. "You mean the one above the restaurant?"

Sissy nodded. "That's right."

"But it isn't even on the schedule yet. No one told us the chef was supposed to live there." Quinn glanced momentarily at Eloise. "I'm sorry, miss, but the apartment renovation won't be ready for months."

"Months?" She hadn't meant for her voice to jump an octave or two.

Over the next few minutes, everyone spoke at once. The two sisters explaining to the Farraday's Aunt Eileen about the Red Hat ladies, and an upcoming quilting convention, and what a bloody mess the council had gotten them into by not telling them about the new chef needing two rooms, not one.

Aunt Eileen's eyes sparkled with interest. "And your brother will be here when?"

"About three weeks, and as the Sisters have explained, there won't be a spare room available for him."

Now, the big gray dog that reminded Eloise a bit of a wolf stood and moved to her side as if offering comfort for the rooming problem.

"Well." Her gaze focused on the dog at Eloise's feet, a slight smile teased at the corners of the older woman's mouth as she straightened. A determined gaze leveled with Eloise's. "Seems there's only one solution. You'll both stay with us at the ranch."

Quinn's head snapped up. "Aunt Eileen—"

Ignoring her nephew's protest, Eileen addressed Eloise. "I'm sorry there was a scheduling mistake, but we have plenty of room at the ranch for you and your brother."

Eloise blinked. "That's very kind, but—"

"No buts. It's the most logical solution. You can ride to work every day with the boys here, or borrow a ranch vehicle. As long as you don't mind old trucks."

"Well, no, but—"

Sporting a full on grin, Aunt Eileen clapped her hands

together. "Then it's settled. As soon as you're done with the kitchen here, Quinn will collect your things and bring you back to the ranch."

"Me?" Quinn's eyebrows rose.

"Yes." Aunt Eileen stared at him. "You."

"But Danny won't be here for three weeks, I don't need to move just yet. Besides, maybe the schedule can be rearranged, for the apartment I mean." This whole situation had Eloise a tad confused and a whole lot worried.

"No matter, dear." Aunt Eileen patted her arm. "No sense in settling in twice, besides, the Parlor House is lovely, but it's not a home."

And just like that, everyone went back to their duties, not an argument among them. Eloise had the distinct feeling that everyone knew better than to argue with Aunt Eileen.

By day's end, the once neat and clean restaurant was again mussed from a hard day's work. At least there was no denying the progress they'd made. Eloise had gone over every detail of the kitchen layout once, twice and then again. She gave new meaning to the old adage, measure twice, cut once. Making notes and suggesting minor tweaks, all was accomplished with a persistent smile that somehow made even criticism feel like praise.

Quinn wasn't totally sure what he'd expected from the new chef, but man or woman, Eloise was not it. Once she'd finished her analysis, her requests, and a shopping list as long as his arm, she rolled up her sleeves and joined the rest of the crew in their daily clean up. All the while, her smile never slipping. Now she stood on the sidewalk beside his truck, her small suitcase looking lost in the bed among his tools.

"Ready?" Quinn opened the passenger door, trying not to notice how the setting sun caught golden highlights in her hair.

"As ready as I'm going to be." Already climbing in, she

somehow managed to look both professional and endearingly uncertain. "I really don't like being an imposition, but somehow I got the feeling there was no refusing your aunt."

"If your cooking is as good as your instincts, the restaurant is going to be a big hit."

"She's that difficult?" How the woman could manage looking happy and worried at the same time, he had no clue.

"I don't think difficult is the right word. When there's trouble on the horizon, there isn't anyone better you want on your side than Aunt Eileen, but when the woman makes up her mind, there is no changing it."

"I see." Fastening her seat belt, she heaved a deep sigh.

An overwhelming urge to reach over and stroke her hand and assure her all would be well was almost too strong to hold back. Almost. "Don't let her scare you, she's just a protective mama bear."

The drive to the ranch started quietly. Quinn could feel the nerves radiating from Eloise clear across the cab of his truck, but danged if tongue tied him knew what to say.

"Gray is a sweet dog," she finally broke the silence.

When Gray first met Eloise, he'd sniffed every inch of her pant leg before settling happily at her side, then he pretty much followed Eloise around until a little later when Aunt Eileen made it clear to the ranch canine that it was time to go. Quinn had to admit, though obedient, the dog didn't look very happy to be going home with the family matriarch, leaving his new friend behind.

"Your family seems pretty big," she continued.

"I'm one of six brothers."

"No girls?"

He shook his head. "To my mother's chagrin, no. But now that most of my brothers are married, she's sort of happy to have daughters-in-law."

"Sort of?" One brow rose higher than the other in the cutest little expression of confusion.

"We're all in Texas, she and Dad are in Oklahoma. She's not too happy about that."

"I suppose I could understand why. They don't want to move?"

"My dad probably would. He'd been estranged from his brother and cousin—that would be Uncle Sean—but now that they've mended fences, I think he would be happy to be in the fold again."

"And your mother?"

His mother. That was a question they'd all been asking themselves and still didn't have an answer for. "Let's say not so much."

"Do you think you and your brothers are going to stay in Texas?"

A year or so ago, he probably would have said not likely; now, he felt the Farraday roots as strong as that of a two-hundred-year-old live oak tree—he and his brothers weren't going anywhere. "My family has been in Texas since before Texas was Texas."

"Must be nice." She still sported a smile, but a hint of sadness showed through.

If he could think of a way to ask more without prying, he would have. Normally, he could not care less what people's stories were, but today he really wanted to know why her tone was so sad. Actually, even more surprising, he sort of wanted to fix it too.

"Well, if you're okay with everyone in your space and your business, it's just peachy."

"So, you don't like it?"

Did he? His face spread with what might have been his first smile of the day. "I wouldn't have it any other way."

"I think I knew you were going to say that."

Before he could respond, he slowed as they approached the ranch entrance. "Your welcoming committee awaits." Uncle Sean and his cousin Connor stood talking on the front porch. From the number of cars and trucks parked nearby, Quinn was pretty sure that Aunt Eileen had called in the troops for a family dinner even if it wasn't Sunday.

"More family?" Something in Eloise's voice made Quinn glance over. He couldn't testify to it in a court of law, but he felt sure he saw longing in her eyes, quickly hidden behind that sunny smile.

"Anywhere near Tuckers Bluff, you can't turn around

without tripping over a Farraday."

"Sadieville too?" Her voice sounded a bit more timid than it had earlier in the day. He suspected the number of Farradays coming onto the porch to greet them was making her a bit nervous.

"Getting that way."

Someone opened the screen door just enough for Gray to run out, making a beeline for Connor's young son playing in front. The boy's delighted laughter echoed across the yard.

"And the chaos begins." Quinn helped Eloise down from the truck. The scent of his aunt's famous pot roast drifted from the house, along with the sound of multiple conversations and what seemed to be a heated debate about baseball.

"Quinn!" Connor called from the porch. "Aunt Eileen said you were bringing our new chef. Come on up—Dad's about to tell the story about the ghost horse again."

"Ghost horse?" Eloise whispered.

"Family legend. It's why the first Farraday in the new country decided to propose to an American bride."

"He needed a ghost horse to propose?"

Quinn shrugged. "From what I remember, my however many greats ago grandfather left Ireland to earn money to send for his bride. Before he could do that, she got sick and died. He felt guilty for years. He swore the ghost horse was the spirit of his first wife telling him to keep living without her, so he proposed and the rest, as they say, is history."

"That's sweet." Eloise heaved a sigh, straightened her shoulders, and marched to the porch steps.

Quinn watched his family's easy embrace of their house guest. Connor's wife was already pulling Eloise into a conversation about Chicago restaurants, while Aunt Eileen explained about her having Grace's old room and how much she was going to love it. Already he could see the tension in Eloise's shoulders easing. Maybe everything would work out just fine, even if there was no way in hell that apartment was getting done any time soon.

CHAPTER FIVE

The aroma of fresh coffee filled the ranch kitchen as dawn painted the horizon in watercolor hues. Eloise had expected a basic country kitchen, not this massive space with top-of-the-line appliances, quartz countertops, and enough room to feed an army. Which, given the number of Farradays she'd met last night and how many were still left to meet, probably wasn't far off.

She glanced around in search of the dog who had been her shadow most of last evening. Allowing her to scratch behind his ears had been as soothing for Eloise as for the dog. The other dog that was clearly Gray's favorite companion, came over from time to time for a little scratch or sniff, but the big gray dog was the one who remained mostly at her side, or comfortably in a corner, his tail thumping against the hardwood floor each time she passed.

"Good morning." Aunt Eileen stood at the sink, smiling over her shoulder. "Did you sleep well?"

After the best night's sleep she'd had in months—courtesy of the cloud-soft bed in what Aunt Eileen called "Grace's old room"—Eloise felt energized. "Very well, thank you. The room is just lovely. And the view."

The bedroom itself had been a revelation. Soft blues and creams, a window seat perfect for reading, and a view that stretched forever across the Texas landscape.

"Wait till you see the sunset." Aunt Eileen reached for another dirty dish. "Best view of the setting sun, other than the back porch."

She'd caught the hues of a rising sun when she passed through the living room, and she could hardly wait to catch sunset.

"I'm just about to fix the second round of breakfast."

"Second round?" She thought she'd risen bright and early.

Aunt Eileen nodded. "Sean and the hands are already out working."

"Oh, is that where Gray is?"

"Yes ma'am. Best cattle dog a rancher could ask for." Eileen reached for a bowl and a griddle. "Now it's time to feed the construction crew, and anyone who skipped the first breakfast but is ready to fuel up."

"What's on the menu?" Eloise watched the woman pull out pans and plates and ingredients from the massive fridge.

"Just eggs, bacon, and fresh biscuits. If the mood moves me, I might make some pancakes too."

"Allow me." Eloise didn't wait for approval, she opened the fridge and began pulling out ingredients. "I make a mean French toast breakfast casserole."

The way Aunt Eileen stared at her, for a moment panic rushed through her, fearing she'd offended the woman.

A slow smile took over the older woman's face as she grabbed a rag and wiped her hands. "That may be the best offer I've had all year. Besides, how stupid would I have to be to fight a professional chef for control of a kitchen?"

"Oh, I didn't mean to—." That panic in the pit of her stomach was growing.

"No, dear." Aunt Eileen set her hand on Eloise's forearm. "It's always a blessing to have help in the kitchen. What would you like me to do?"

By the time boot heels were stomping down the stairs, fresh biscuits filled the warming drawer, bacon crisped on the griddle, and she'd just pulled her brother's favorite breakfast casserole from the oven.

"Something smells amazing." Quinn's deep voice carried from the doorway, still gravelly with sleep.

She turned to find him in worn jeans and a faded t-shirt, his hair still damp from a morning shower, looking far too appealing for this early hour. "I hope you're hungry."

"Always." He poured two cups of coffee, sliding one toward her. "You didn't have to do this."

"Consider it a thank you for the room. And the welcome." She accepted the coffee, their fingers brushing briefly, her awareness of him escalating unexpectedly.

"I offer my hearty *you're very welcome* on behalf of everyone eating breakfast this morning." He took a long slow sip of coffee before looking up at her. "Did you sleep well?"

"Best sleep in a long time. Grace has good taste."

"She loved that room. Aunt Eileen moved in with the family when her sister died after giving birth to Grace. Back then, we only spent summers in Texas, but I still remember Aunt Eileen and Grace picking out all the colors and fabrics. Somehow they made it feel like it wasn't just the two of them decorating, but Aunt Helen as well. Grace said that's why sleeping in that room was like sleeping with the angels."

"She's right." Sleeping with angels was exactly how she'd felt.

Within minutes, Ryan had joined them. Followed by Paxton, another brother who still lived with the Farradays but would be marrying soon and moving to a house of their own in town. Before more than a hello or two was shared, the kitchen door opened and Connor came in, stomping his boots. "Man, something smells good."

Aunt Eileen grinned, lifting her chin, beaming with pride as if she'd been the one to make the breakfast. "Eloise made a special breakfast casserole."

"Really?" Connor pulled out his phone and within minutes his wife Catherine, who was originally from Chicago like her, their daughter and young son were on their way over.

"Well now, I don't know about you, but I'm awfully glad the town council screwed up and your apartment isn't ready yet." Aunt Eileen surveyed the spread with approval. "Not that I expect you to cook for us, but this is indeed a wonderful way to start the morning." The woman spun about and pulled Eloise into a tight hug before stepping back. "Thank you."

A chorus of *thank you* from everyone at the table met

her ears along with mutterings of more eggs please, save some for me, and danged these are amazing biscuits.

Eloise felt warmth spread through her chest that had nothing to do with the ovens. So this is what it meant to have a family. Too bad they weren't hers.

Sunlight streamed through the kitchen windows as Quinn, lingering for no particular reason, savored his third cup of coffee. Most of the family had cleared out, heading to their respective jobs and responsibilities. Even Aunt Eileen had disappeared, lugging a basket of clean laundry to hang on the line. Despite their having a perfectly good dryer, his aunt preferred hanging the laundry the old-fashioned way on sunny days.

Eloise hummed softly while loading the dishwasher. He'd offered to help more than once, but her insistence that she had it under control reminded him of his aunt. Cleaning up, she'd moved with the same efficiency she'd shown while cooking. He'd noticed that about her—everything she did had purpose, even if she made it look effortless.

"Are you wanting to go back to the construction site, or would you rather stay here and settle in?" He rinsed his cup and set it in the rack she'd just filled.

"I'd like to go with you. There are a few more things I need to work out; besides there's not that much to settle in here." She closed the dishwasher, wiped her hands on a towel. "Though I need to figure out my own transportation soon. I can't keep depending on you for rides."

"What's this?" Aunt Eileen came back, dropping the empty basket on the counter.

"I need to work on getting a vehicle of my own to get back and forth to Sadieville, or into Tuckers Bluff."

"Remember…" Quinn leaned against the counter; this was his chance to actually help her. "We've got a few ranch vehicles that don't see much use. No reason not to drive one of ours."

"Like I said before," his aunt paused and faced Eloise, "as long as you don't need pretty."

Quinn nodded, his gaze level with Eloise's. "The blue Ford usually sits idle unless we're moving hay."

Her eyes lit up. "If you're sure, that would be great."

"We're halfway between Tuckers Bluff and Sadieville. The ride to town is pretty smooth, but the ride to the construction site can be a bit bumpy."

"I noticed." That sunny smile appeared again.

"A truck makes more sense than a car."

"I may have learned to drive in Chicago, but I can't imagine navigating the dirt roads in a low riding sedan."

The woman was strong, sweet, and sensible too. Suddenly, he felt an odd loss at the thought of not riding together. "For now, why don't we carpool until you learn your way?"

Her head tipped to one side. "Is that Texan for GPS doesn't work out here?"

"Something like that." He couldn't help but chuckle.

"Thought so." She nodded, gathering her bag with what looked like several notebooks and a laptop.

The morning air still held a hint of cool as they stepped outside. By the end of the day, the sun would make everything feel like an oven. Holding the passenger door open for her, his mind started churning with what comes next. "Your brother arrives in three weeks?"

"Twenty days." The immediate response told him she'd been counting. "The VA clinic in Midland already has his paperwork, and his therapy team in Chicago thinks the change will be good for him."

Quinn nodded, turning onto the ranch road. "Uncle Sean mentioned that if your brother wants some busy work, we'd be happy to let him work with the barn animals. Said something about how working with your hands can help clear the mind."

He caught her quick glance, the slight shine in her eyes before she blinked it away. "That's... that's very kind."

"That's Uncle Sean." What he didn't know for sure was what exactly her brother's situation was. Eloise mentioned at dinner that her brother had done three tours in the military and that he was doing therapy, but she didn't say much more, though her concern for her brother could be easily seen in her eyes. "I don't mean to pry, but do you think working with horses would help your brother?"

"Horses? Are those the barn animals your uncle wants him to work with?"

"Oh. No. I was thinking about my cousin Hannah. You haven't met her yet, she's in Dallas visiting some friends for the long weekend. She's an equine therapist. Works out of Connor's place. She works with kids and veterans, and has done some amazing work," Quinn clarified.

"Oh, I don't know, but I can certainly look into it."

Quinn nodded. "You can talk to Hannah when she comes home."

"I'd like that."

"And here we go again." He slowed the truck and pointed ahead. Four cows strolled, very slowly, across the road.

"I gather this happens often?"

"Unfortunately, the Brady's cattle break through their fence every other Tuesday."

"You're joking." Her laugh filled the cab of the truck, and something in his chest tightened at the sound.

"Wish I was. Those cows have a standing appointment with freedom."

By the time they reached the construction site, she had three pages of notes about local roads, landmarks, and yes, the Brady's escape-artist cattle. Quinn couldn't remember the last time a simple drive to work had been so entertaining.

Or maybe it wasn't the drive at all.

CHAPTER SIX

An unexpected surge of excitement shot through Eloise as Quinn pulled up to the restaurant. For every inch of her that prayed this move was the right thing for herself and her brother, there was another inch terrified this would be the biggest mistake of her life. After less than twenty-four hours in West Texas, her fears had completely disappeared and enthusiasm for what was to come continued to build.

Standing on the front porch, Quinn reached for Eloise's arm. "Listen."

It took everything in her not to jump at his touch. "Yes?"

"Ryan, Morgan, and the crew are already hard at work in the dining room." Quinn nodded toward the rhythmic sound of hammering. "If you want to take a look at the apartment space, now would be a good time."

"Really?" Her heart did a little two step. Even though she was settling in at the ranch, she couldn't help being excited over a sneak peek at what would be her home.

Quinn led her down a narrow alley and a staircase leading up to a faded gray door. "Watch your step. We came up here when checking out the beams but didn't fix any of the soft spots on the stairs."

The steps creaked under their feet, the sound echoing in her ears against the thudding of every heartbeat. At the top, Quinn pushed open the door, and Eloise stepped into the surprisingly spacious room, and back in time about a hundred or so years.

Sunlight filtered through grimy windows, catching the dust they'd stirred up. The space was huge—spanning from back to front of the building. Strips of old wallpaper, probably stylish in its time, hung peeled from the walls after decades of stifling heat and humidity. In one corner, an ancient cast-iron wood-burning stove stood sentinel.

"Oh my goodness." Eloise moved toward the stove, running her hand over its surface. "This is a Monarch 6210. They were the cream of the crop in the early 1900s."

Pulling a flashlight from his pocket, Quinn flashed the beam on the old appliance. "You know about antique stoves?"

"My first restaurant job, the owner collected them." She opened one of the oven doors carefully. "This one's completely intact. With a little restoration effort, it could probably still work."

"Here's something else you might like." Quinn moved to a corner, illuminating what looked like an old cabinet.

As Eloise drew closer, she saw the old freestanding cabinet was actually a Hoosier. Aged oak with a slate top and the original flour sifter still attached. "The woman who lived here must have loved to cook." Eloise opened one of the cabinet doors, revealing a collection of ancient utensils. "Holy dairy. A butter mold. And a nutmeg grinder."

"I know the kitchen is your domain, but do people still use these things?" Quinn's gaze danced from one ancient utensil to the other.

She shrugged. "I doubt most people even know what they are, but as far back as I can remember, I've always loved cooking. Watched cooking shows on television as a kid, and eventually got hooked on antique shows. Oddities like this always came up. I even have a few boxed up and in storage from when I had time to hit estate sales and antique shops."

"I look forward to seeing your collections some day."

Surprised by the comment, she turned to see him better in the dimly lit room. Sincerity sparkled in his eyes. Had she ever known anyone who cared one lick about antique kitchen tools? She didn't know what to make of the gruff man with few words, but she wouldn't mind learning more. Spinning around, she reached for what she thought was an old coffee grinder. "Oh, wow. It still has beans in it."

Quinn leaned closer, his presence warm at her shoulder. "I guess they've been preserved in time since the town went bust."

Scanning the sparse dust covered, furnishings she shook her head. "It's like somebody just walked away one day and never came back."

"Or maybe," he hefted a lazy shoulder, "the ghosts like it."

"Ghosts?"

Now he had to resist the urge to chuckle at her startled reaction. "It is a ghost town."

"Yeah, but no one said anything about real ghosts." Turning slowly, she took in the whole space with such intensity that he wondered if she thought he was serious. "Ghosts." With a quick bob of her head, she huffed out a deep breath and shifted to face him. "Okay let's see the rest of it."

Carefully following her, Quinn took his time, stopping when she stopped, leaning over for a closer look at anything that interested her. When she walked into a third room with an intact bedroom suite, including an old armoire and vanity set, she almost lost her breath.

Stopping at the dresser, Quinn opened one of the drawers. "Well crafted. You don't see furniture like this anymore. No nails. Dove tails fit together perfectly. Fascinating."

"There's a lot to do, isn't there?"

Quinn nodded. "First and foremost, we have to carve out a couple of bathrooms. You'll want more than an armoire for closets, so most of these walls will have to be taken down and moved."

"Bathrooms would be nice." She flashed a toothy grin at him. "And closets would be appreciated too, but I want to keep the Monarch and the Hoosier. They deserve to be part of the new space."

Quinn's chuckle was warm in the musty air. "They'll need to be restored if you're going to actually use them."

"I'm not sure I know where to begin, but," she smiled

up at him, "every home should have a piece of history, don't you think?"

His gaze leveled with hers and he stared at her for so long with such intensity, she wondered what the man was thinking. Finally, his lips parted and he muttered, "Things of beauty need to be cherished."

His voice came out low and deep, and sounded smooth as melted butter. What she didn't know was whether he was referring to the kitchen or something else. Without moving, his gaze remained fixed on her and she had an overwhelming urge to stand in his personal space and see what he would do. Except the sound of his brothers calling up the stairs broke the moment.

Quinn cleared his throat. "We should head down. The salvaged hardwood floors for the dining room are due to be delivered any minute. That's probably what those two yahoos are hollering about."

Nodding, Eloise took a step in retreat and then followed him out the door. As they descended the stairs, she cast one last look up at the apartment. Life was looking really good—in so many ways. Oh how she hoped Danny was going to love this place as much as she already did. Then again, maybe it would be nicer to have a little house with a view of the sunset, and maybe even better, a tall dark and handsome cowboy—or carpenter—to go with it.

"I'll see your five and raise you five." Eileen Callahan Farraday tossed a few chips into the pot. Having Eloise in the house to help with breakfast and clean up had helped her get to town early enough to join in on the Tuckers Bluff Ladies Afternoon Social Club's biweekly card game at the café.

Ruth Ann raised one brow at her long-time friend. "I think you're bluffing. See your five."

An echo of "I'm in" moved around the table.

Dorothy, Declan Farraday's grandmother-in-law, folded

her cards and tapped them lightly on the table. "What I want to know is what's this new chef like?"

"I told you," Eileen tossed two cards onto the table. "Nice."

"Nice," Sally May said with a sigh. "We want more than that."

Eileen shrugged. "She's a good cook."

"Or course she's a good cook," Dorothy hissed. "She's a chef."

Unable to hold back her amusement at teasing her old friends, Eileen cracked a smile and set her cards face down on the table. "All right."

All of her friends leaned in closer over the table in the corner of the café as if Eileen were about to reveal national secrets. "She's petite, has blonde hair cropped just above her shoulders, pretty blue eyes, and smiles like there's no tomorrow."

Ruth Ann bobbed her head. "So she's nice," the woman teased back.

"Told ya!" Eileen winked and burst into laughter before clearing her throat to continue. "She's also a damn good cook. I mean, all I've tasted is her breakfast, but that casserole she made was to die for. I've never seen all my men shovel food so fast in my life."

"Well, that's a relief." Dorothy picked up her cards. "I was afraid the council was going to hire some fancy French chef with a heavy accent, a flair for the dramatic, and haute cuisine like snails and raw beef on the menu."

"It's not raw," Ruth Ann rolled her eyes, "it's *tartar*."

"Whatever." Dorothy stared at her cards a moment before returning her attention to Eileen. "Any chance she'll take to one of your boys?"

It always made Eileen smile how in her and her friend's eyes, her grown nephews were still boys. "I'm thinking so."

"Your eyes are sparkling." Ruth Ann studied her. "Which one is tripping over himself? Quinn or Ryan?"

"Not sure yet."

"Oh?" Dorothy tipped her head. "Is she drooling over one of the boys?"

Eileen shook her head.

"Then what is it?" Sally May huffed.

Leaning forward more, Eileen looked around their table then still smiling, let her gaze dart from friend to friend. "Gray is glued to her side!"

All her friends leaned back in their seats, clapped their hands and giggled like schoolgirls. Dorothy was the one to squeal, "Looks like another Farraday wedding on the horizon."

Following Eloise to the front of the building, Quinn paused at the sound of the delivery crew arguing over who should put the hardwood planks where. Shaking his head at them, he continued up the porch steps, their voices faded into the background noise as his mind lingered on the apartment tour.

The way Eloise's eyes had lit up at each discovery wouldn't leave him. How naturally she'd rattled off details about antique kitchen tools that he'd assumed were just junk. Her excitement over the Monarch stove had been contagious—he'd already decided to talk to Connie, Neil's decorator wife, about having it restored. Somewhere on one of their past jobs back in Oklahoma, he remembered her having a restoration specialist who could take the ugliest piece of garbage and make it look—and work—like showroom new.

"Earth to Quinn." Morgan's voice broke through his thoughts. "Do you care where they put these boards?"

Quinn blinked, forcing his mind back to the task at hand. "Stack them along the east wall. They need to acclimate to the space before installation."

Morgan rolled his eyes at his brother and walked away muttering, "Tell us something we don't already know."

Addressing the delivery people, Quinn extended his arm. "Pile the planks along that far wall, out of the way of our current working area." One eye on the men stacking the wood, the rest of his mind was already mentally sketching what he himself would do to bring that old Hoosier cabinet back to life. He couldn't remember the last time he'd been this excited about a project. All he hoped was that Eloise liked surprises.

CHAPTER SEVEN

The ranch kitchen buzzed with activity as Eloise pulled another pan of rolls from the oven. Cars and trucks had been arriving ever since church ended, the sounds of greetings and laughter drifted throughout the large family home. Ever since she'd found out that she would be awarded the position of head chef at the new restaurant, she'd been playing around with ideas for the menu. In the few days she'd been here, the Sisters had let her try out a few ideas in the Parlor's kitchen. Now, Aunt Eileen had agreed to let her use the family for guinea pigs this afternoon.

"Something smells amazing." Hannah appeared in the doorway, her dark hair pulled back in a neat braid. "Aunt Eileen said you're testing new dishes on us."

"Your aunt insisted." Eloise checked her tried and true specialty, beef bourguignon, simmering on the stove. "I hope that's okay."

"Are you kidding? We never turn down good food." Hannah flashed a toothy grin. "Need any help?"

Before Eloise could answer, more family members crowded the kitchen doorway. Meg, Adam's wife, carried a tray of Toni's cake balls. She was probably more excited to taste the cake balls that the entire town raved about than the family was to taste her food.

Smiling brightly, a slim blonde carried a large platter in her hand with four small children running circles around her. "Hey, no one wants me to drop Aunt Eileen's favorite platter. Either slow down or take it outside."

Eloise had done her best to keep a run down on who was who, but there were just too many names for her to remember everyone.

"Hi there, I'm Becky, Declan's wife."

"Eloise."

"Oh, my." Becky set the platter down on the kitchen table. "This looks like quite the feast cooking. Not to mention the kitchen smells heavenly!"

"Thank you."

The four kids that had been circling hurried around the table then ran past them and out the door just as Becky shouted, "Don't slam"—*bang*—"the door behind you."

Eloise chuckled at the I-give-up expression on the woman's face. "Are they all yours?"

Becky's eyes rounded like silver dollars. "Heaven's no. Connor, Jamison, Adam, and us all had kids within months of each other. Only the blonde with the long ponytail is mine."

Just as Connor's wife Catherine crossed into the kitchen, Aunt Eileen hurried in behind her. "Out, all of you. Let the woman work. Shoo!"

Laughing and chatting, the women slowly retreated, each one pairing off with their spouses. Eloise took a moment to absorb it all. The whole big crazy family was something foster kids dreamed of, but even in her wildest of imaginations, she'd never come up with a family quite like the Farradays.

"Sorry about that." Aunt Eileen winked. "They're just excited. We haven't had a professional chef cook Sunday dinner since… well, ever."

Stirring her sauce, Eloise added a pinch more thyme. "I just hope it lives up to expectations."

"Oh honey," Aunt Eileen squeezed her shoulder and smiled, "you passed those the first morning you made breakfast. Now you're just showing off."

The sound of children's laughter echoed from outside, followed by the deeper rumble of men's voices. Her heart squeezed, imagining Danny here in little more than a week, part of this warm chaos. He'd always been the one taking care of her, even when his own world was falling apart. Now maybe she could finally give him something he desperately needed—a place to heal.

"You've outdone yourself." Aunt Eileen surveyed the kitchen. The rolls filled three baskets, and a chocolate bourbon pecan pie—her grandmother's recipe—cooled on the counter.

To go with the beef, Eloise had kept things simple with her signature dishes. "I wanted to try different things, something for everyone's taste," Eloise explained. "The beef with rosemary roasted potatoes, fresh green beans with toasted almonds, and honey-glazed carrots is my sure thing. We'll also have Chicken Roulade—stuffed with spinach, sun-dried tomatoes and goat cheese, served with a white wine sauce, or blackened redfish with crawfish cream sauce. For the sides, there's roasted corn soufflé and Gruyere and green chili scalloped potatoes."

"Wow. You're spoiling us." Aunt Eileen nodded approvingly. "Though I suspect you could serve shoe leather and this bunch would eat it if you made the sauce." She straightened her shoulders and reached for serving dishes. "Time to get this show on the road."

Whenever she cooked, she was in her own little section of heaven. Nothing could faze her. Suddenly, she was racked with doubts. Maybe she should have chosen all comfort standards. Maybe this part of the country wouldn't appreciate goat cheese and whole fat French Gruyere. And maybe she should stop second-guessing herself.

"Ready?" Aunt Eileen picked up the bowl with the beef bourguignon.

Eloise surveyed her dishes one last time. Her favorite foster mother used to always tell her, *fake it till you make it*. Those words had brought her this far. Ready or not, there was no turning back now. Picking up the platter of fish, she turned to face Aunt Eileen. "Let's do it."

Finn and his wife Joanna came hurrying into the dining room, each carrying a platter of food from the kitchen.

"Sorry we're late." Finn set one platter on the buffet behind him.

Joanna sniffed at the air. "I haven't smelled so many delicious aromas in my life. My mouth has been watering since I hit the kitchen door."

The sound of chairs scraping the hardwood floors bounced against the family chatter as folks hurried into the kitchen to help carry out the remainder of the food.

The massive dining table groaned under the weight of Eloise's feast. Quinn wasn't sure if he'd ever seen this much food, not even at Thanksgiving. Everything smelled amazing. Already his brothers were eyeing the arriving platters like hungry wolves.

Food began circulating, accompanied by appreciative murmurs and the clink of serving spoons. Quinn couldn't remember the last time his normally boisterous family had been too busy eating to talk. Even the kids were eating the vegetables without complaint. Quinn shouldn't have been surprised, he'd already eaten the few things that Eloise had cooked at the ranch and knew she was a fabulous cook. No, not just a cook—a chef.

"Do we have a date for when we can all descend on the restaurant and try out the rest of your menu?" Catherine took the last bite of her chicken.

"That depends on staffing," Eloise answered. "I'll need at least two solid line cooks, prep staff, servers. Plus time to train everyone the way I want the kitchen to run."

Aunt Eileen reached for another roll. "Are you a hard task master like that television chef who comes in and saves failing restaurants?"

"I hope not." She chuckled, her cheeks pinkened, her eyes sparkled, and Quinn almost swallowed his tongue.

"Which reminds me." Ryan stabbed at a piece of his corn soufflé. "The kitchen equipment arrives tomorrow."

The way Eloise's eyes lit up brought a smile to Quinn's lips.

"What are you grinning at?" Ryan held his fork in mid-air.

All eyes turned in the direction Ryan was staring.

"What? Is it against the law to smile?" Quinn said.

"No." One corner of Ryan's mouth twitched with a hint of amusement.

"Hm." Quinn grunted, returning his attention to the food on his plate. Ignoring all the eyes on him, he noticed his aunt watching him the most intently, not missing any of the discussion, or probably the smiles.

Still watching him to the point of making him want to shift in his seat—or better yet, hide under the table—Aunt Eileen shared a smile with her husband before turning back to Eloise. "I saw the help wanted signs for the restaurant up at the hardware store and the Cut n' Curl."

Becky dabbed at the corners of her mouth. "I saw them up at the café and O'Faredeigh's."

Eloise nodded, her grin bright. "I already have staffing interviews lined up tomorrow morning."

"Ooh, that could be fun." Valerie, ever the producer, chimed in. "We'll film all the interviews for the show, then air the ones who are actually hired. The ratings will eat it up."

Morgan closed his knife and fork on the plate he'd come short of licking clean. "I don't see how the ratings can get any higher."

"Now, now, no talk of ratings tonight." Aunt Eileen pushed away from the table. "There's dessert in the kitchen."

"Let me get it." Eloise stood.

His aunt looked ready to protest, and before she could object, Quinn pushed to his feet. "You can sit, Aunt Eileen. I'll help Eloise."

There was no need to look over his shoulder, he could feel his aunt's gaze on his back as he followed Eloise into the kitchen.

"I left the pies cooling over here." She went straight to the butler's pantry.

The way Eloise moved about in the kitchen, she looked like someone who had lived at the ranch her whole life, especially her ability to cook for a massive clan of people. Of course, she obviously did that every night in her line of work. Still, somehow the idea of her being well suited to ranch life sat well with him. And wasn't that absurd. What she was suited for was none of his business.

"Here you go." She handed him two pies, one for each hand.

"I sure hope you have more than this. You may think that crowd is full, but don't let looks deceive you."

Her eyes sparkled with delight. "There's a lot more where those came from." Her fingers landed on the back of his shoulder. "Go on. I'll be right there with two more pies."

Like a branding iron, he could feel the heat of her touch through his clothing, searing his skin. His tongue seemed to be stuck to the roof of his mouth so he nodded, forcing his feet to move, one in front of the other, wondering why did this woman make him feel so…different.

Setting the two pies down in the middle of the massive dining table, he made room for the additional pies. To his surprise, not only had Eloise cooked dinner and baked pies, she turned on her heel and returned with homemade ice cream.

"You made ice cream too?" Uncle Sean seemed beyond impressed.

"She had help." The love in Aunt Eileen's eyes softened her words.

The conversation bounced around, from talk of the new calves, to the superb dinner, to the upcoming arrival of Eloise's brother next week. Heavy chatter just like any other Sunday evening dinner, and yet, gourmet food aside, nothing about tonight felt normal. Nothing at all.

CHAPTER EIGHT

Sleep proved impossible. Eloise tossed and turned, her mind racing with a mix of excitement and anxiety. Progress at the restaurant since Sunday dinner had been energizing. The kitchen turned out even better than she'd imagined—every piece of equipment precisely where it needed to be, precisely what she'd hoped for. Her first two hires seemed perfect: Sarah, a local girl with three years of experience at the café, and Miguel, who'd worked in some impressive kitchens in Dallas before moving here with his young family.

But thoughts of Danny's arrival next week kept chasing away any chance of rest. Her brother had been her best friend and protector for as long as she could remember, and now, the role reversal since his return home was still new territory for her. Would he like it here? Would the quiet help or make things worse? Was it possible that the equine therapy center run by Hannah could make a true difference in Danny's struggle?

Giving up on sleep, she slipped from bed and pulled on her robe. The house was silent except for the distant hum of crickets. She made her way downstairs, drawn to the back porch where Aunt Eileen claimed the sunset views could cure any trouble. This late, the sunset was long gone, but taking a few minutes to sway back and forth in the large green rockers that lined the back porch, and simply relax among the crickets and stars, made more sense than continuing to toss and turn.

Settled comfortably in the rocker closest to the corner, she already appreciated the light show of stars above her. Aunt Eileen had been right. Even without the setting sun, the stars flickering in the distant sky was as relaxing as any sunny day. Taking a moment to glance around, she noticed a distant light glowed from one of the outbuildings. Curious, she stepped off the porch. She felt thankful she'd fished her rubber soled slippers out from under the bed rather than head to the kitchen barefoot as she might have done otherwise.

Slowly, she made her way down the pebbled path. At the building, the door stood partially open, and the rhythmic sound of sandpaper against wood drifted out. Quinn sat on a work stool, carefully smoothing the arm of a rocking chair.

"Couldn't sleep either?" she asked softly.

He looked up, not seeming surprised to see her. "It's for Aunt Eileen's birthday."

"It's beautiful." She stepped closer, admiring the chair's graceful lines. "Are you refinishing it?"

He shook his head. "Not this time. She loves antiques. My original plan was to find an old one in a barn somewhere—there's always old furniture stored in lofts in this part of Texas—but never came across one that seemed right, so…"

"You made this?" She hadn't meant for her voice to sound so surprised.

"I did." He nodded. "I'm almost done.

The warm golden wood gleamed in the workshop's light. "When is her birthday?"

"Not till next month, but I didn't want to rush."

Running her hands over the bowed back, she couldn't help but marvel at his craftsmanship. She already knew he could raise a wall or build a cabinet with the best of them, but this, this was something special. "She'll love it."

"Hope so." He set aside the sandpaper. "What's keeping you up?"

"Everything. Nothing." She perched on the edge of his workbench. "The kitchen's perfect, so far I'm really happy with the people we've hired, but…"

"Danny?"

She nodded, surprised and yet somewhat pleased that he seemed to know what was worrying her. "I keep wondering if I'm doing the right thing. The city had become too much for him. He wanted to get away, but is moving us all the way out here just to escape Chicago's noise and crowds overkill?"

Quinn was quiet for a moment, his hands resting on the chair's arm. "Well, you know there are no crowds, and not a lot of noise, around here. Sometimes the right thing doesn't feel right until after you've done it."

The workshop scents of sawdust and furniture polish added to the feeling of comforting peace. "What's that?" She pushed to her feet and crossed over to a pair of candlestick end tables.

"Those are barnyard finds. Thought it would be fun to restore them."

One was already nearly finished. Sturdy, strong, the finish smooth and shiny. The other, held together by clamps, looked like it had sat in too many years of sun and rain. "I guess this one was in worse shape."

He slowly shook his head. "No. The other was worse, that's why I started with it."

Running her fingers against the pristine antiquity and then the scratchy surface of the work in progress, she marveled at the woodwork in this room. A reflection of the man himself. Steady. Reliable. The kind of person who could take broken things and make them whole again. Useful. Beautiful.

"You're close to your brother." Quinn reached for a different grade of sandpaper.

"He's always been there for me. Would always throw just enough of a fit so we wouldn't be separated in the system."

"System?"

"Foster care." Still fingering more of his woodwork, she heard his slight intake of breath. "Danny's probably the reason I made it through foster care. No matter what, he always looked out for me." Somehow, finding the words, sharing the memories, the hurts, came easier in the quiet workshop. "When things got bad, he'd sneak into the kitchen, make me hot chocolate. Even if it was just powder and hot water, he always made it feel special."

Quinn nodded, his hands moving steadily over the wood. "And now it's your turn to take care of him."

"I just hope I'm doing it right." Back at his side, she traced a finger along the chair's smooth arm. "The therapist in Chicago thinks the quiet will help. Says he needs space to breathe."

"Plenty of that here." Quinn looked up, meeting her eyes. "And plenty of people who understand about needing to heal."

Something in his voice made her heart skip, her mind running through how supportive Hannah and Connor had been as well as his cousin Ethan. She watched his hands move over the wood, strong and gentle at the same time. "Thank you."

"For what?"

"For making me feel like maybe I'm not crazy for uprooting everything and coming halfway across the country to a ghost town to start a new life."

The soft smile that stretched across his face seemed to hug her like a warm blanket. "Nothing crazy about wanting to help someone you love."

So the gruff and quiet cowboy had a soft spot. Had she realized that before? Mentally nodding to herself, she knew she had. All the Farraday men were good and honorable, any idiot could see that. But Quinn, he was strong and honorable and gentle and sensitive, and someone she most definitely wanted to get to know better. She could only hope that Danny would take to Farraday country and give her that chance. There was one other thing she was sure of—she really wanted that chance.

Quinn sat perfectly still, watching Eloise's fingers trail over the sanded arm of the rocker. Her touch was gentle, appreciative—the same way she handled ingredients in the kitchen. Like she understood the value of things others might overlook.

A longing to cover her hand with his and share his work more closely surprised him. He wanted to know so much more about her, about her past, her life, her dreams, but he had no idea where to start. "I guess your interest in antiques extends outside the kitchen?"

Her head bobbed as she pulled her hand away from the rocking chair. "Since the council mentioned a furnished apartment, I decided to sell most of my furniture."

"I see," he spoke softly.

"Danny found me a deal on a moving truck already coming to West Texas and had room for a small load. Extra clothes, some of my kitchenware, an old restored dresser."

"You restore furniture?"

She chuckled. "Not me. Danny tried."

"Tried?" Unless it was in pieces, he didn't understand how the word tried came into play.

"He went through this phase of watching DIY videos. Bought this old dresser at a yard sale. Let's just say it didn't end quite the way he expected."

"But you kept it anyway?" It wasn't really a question.

She nodded. "I use it as a nightstand. The bottom drawer sticks and if I tug too hard the front falls off, so I leave it closed."

"Hm," he muttered, mostly so she knew he was listening.

"It's a bit eclectic in its color scheme—"

"Color scheme? He didn't stain it?"

"No. Like I said, it didn't turn out the way he expected, but I loved it nonetheless."

"Because your brother did the work?" Again, not really a question. The answer could be heard by the fondness in her voice when she spoke about her brother. The entire exchange made Quinn want to smile, pull her into a hug, and tell her what a good sister she was. "So he's not very handy?"

"Used to be. Before..." She settled back against a nearby workbench. "He was a combat engineer. Built bridges, cleared roads. Could fix anything that broke down in the field."

That explained a lot. Quinn had seen it before—skilled hands that suddenly couldn't remember their purpose. Maybe his uncle was right, keeping Danny busy at the ranch could be better for him than letting him hibernate in a quiet room.

"He used to love projects." Her voice softened, admiring a wooden cigar box he'd refinished for his dad. "Remember that hot chocolate I mentioned? One Christmas, he rigged up this whole elaborate pulley system between our rooms. Said Santa needed help delivering to foster kids."

Quinn's heart squeezed. He tried imagining young Eloise and her brother, making the best of whatever situation they landed in. "Sounds like he took good care of you."

"Still does. When he's not struggling with his own demons, he checks on me. Calls to make sure I'm eating more than kitchen scraps during prep hours."

Setting aside his tools, Quinn studied the woman perched on his workbench. Strong enough to run a professional kitchen, gentle enough to understand broken things needed time to heal. "The restaurant's going to be something special."

"You think so?" A smile teasing her lips, hope bloomed in her eyes.

"Know so." He gestured to the chair. "Some things, you can see the potential even when they're still rough. Just takes the right person to bring it out."

Her smile in the workshop's light made his chest tight. "You're good at that, aren't you? Seeing the potential in things?"

"Trying to be. I love taking old things and giving them life again." He picked up his sandpaper again, needing something to do with his hands. Focused on the smooth grain of the wood beneath his fingers, he was careful not to meet her eyes. "Maybe… I can show you how?" The silence that followed made him look up.

Her smile could have lit up all of West Texas. "I'd like that."

Their locked gazes lingered a moment longer when Eloise finally slid off the workbench. "It's getting late. I should try to sleep."

"Sweet dreams." Watching her move toward the door, he noticed how she paused to run her hand along the chair's back one more time.

"Quinn?" She turned in the doorway. "Thank you. For listening."

He nodded, not trusting his voice. After she left, he sat in the quiet workshop, thinking about brothers who protected their sisters, about broken things that could be made whole again, and about the way some people just fit perfectly into your life like the last missing piece of a giant jigsaw puzzle. He couldn't help but wonder if she felt the same way.

CHAPTER NINE

The scent of fresh herbs and ripe fruits filled the café parking lot as Eloise made her way through Tuckers Bluff's Saturday farmers market. The cheerful red and white striped awnings fluttered in the morning breeze, shading tables laden with everything from fresh eggs to homemade jam. Children darted between the stalls, many clutching warm cookies from the church ladies bake sale table. The whole scene felt like something from a vintage postcard—pure small-town America at its finest.

Unlike Chicago's crowded urban markets where everyone was in a hurry and vendors would bag, pack, and brush their paid customers along; here vendors chatted with customers, sharing recipes, family news, and laughter like the old friends they clearly were. One woman's tomatoes practically glowed in the morning sun. Once Eloise had a bagful, she not only had ideas for what to do with them, but she knew that these were Abby from the café's favorite tomato, and Carolyn Brown two rows over had the freshest basil to go with them. Her fingers itched to start cooking.

Balancing bags overflowing with herbs, peaches that smelled so ripe she wanted to sit and eat the whole bag on the spot, tomatoes, peppers, zucchini, and snap peas, she paused at the local honey stall. Coming from hives scattered across three counties, the sample of wildflower honey the old man had insisted she try still lingered sweet on her tongue. One more stop at the sweet corn lady's booth and she'd be set.

Smiling, thinking over all the conversations she'd had in the last hour, she felt like she'd been part of this town her whole life. So much information to process: who was expecting twins, whose grandson just made Eagle Scout, and which jam won first prize at the county fair. Every vendor had a story, and they seemed genuinely interested in her plans for the restaurant.

Whistling down the sidewalk to the front of the hardware store where she'd parked the ranch pick up she'd been using, she shifted the bags, wishing she'd brought the rolling cart she used to use for groceries in Chicago. Almost spilling the tomatoes, she quickly lifted her knee, propping it against the truck as she balanced a couple of bags on it while fishing for the keys in her purse.

She really should have just left the keys in her pocket. Trying desperately to hunt in her purse while the dumb thing kept sliding down her arm and threatening to fall to the ground, she dropped her leg and shifted the bags, praying the peaches didn't tumble out and bruise. This was nuts. It shouldn't be so hard to find the dang keys. Propping the bags on one hip and her other knee against the fender, she plopped her purse on the lifted knee and once again searched for the key ring.

"You sure you don't need some help with that?" an unfamiliar male voice asked.

Eloise blinked. Was the voice talking to her or someone else? Shifting her weight ever so slightly, she tried to glance over her shoulder. All she could see was the back of a denim jacket under a massive sack of something.

"Thanks, Chase. If I can't handle a bag of feed, I'm no use to the family."

She'd recognize the second voice anywhere. Quinn Farraday. Focused on the voice, she'd lost her concentration and the bag of tomatoes began to slip from her hip. "Dang it."

No sooner had the word tumbled from her mouth when her purse crashed to the ground and the knee pressed against the fender slipped, throwing her off balance. Arms flailing, her feet scrambling to find purchase, bags toppled over, tomatoes rolled across the sidewalk, the peaches smacked against the concrete and the bunch of fresh basil she'd been particularly excited about took flight.

As her feet slipped out from under her, all she could see was the blue sky above. Panic shot through as she realized there was nothing to grab onto to stop her fall. Like it or not, she was about to kiss the concrete.

What the hell? Quinn had barely stepped out of the hardware store with the fifty-pound bag of feed his uncle had asked him to pick up perched on his shoulder when a sprig of green smacked him in the face. Swiping it away, he heard a screech behind him as he stepped on something squishy. Glancing down, he spotted red balls rolling along the sidewalk. Not balls, tomatoes. And that's when he caught sight of someone flailing around, about to land flat on their back.

Practically hurling the sack off his shoulder, stumbling over peaches, he managed to lunge forward and grab the arms of the woman beside him. Pulling her against him, he spun about, holding her tightly in front of him. Her weight propelled them both backward until tripping over more fruit, he fell, landing splat on the feed bag.

Instinctively, his grip on the warm body now on top of him tightened.

"What happened?" a soft voice spoke. Not any voice, Eloise.

"We fell."

One eyebrow shot up as she stared at him a long moment before turning her attention to survey the situation. "Oh, my peaches." Another second as she looked the other way and her normally sunny disposition faded into a frown. "And the tomatoes."

"Shopping?"

Her attention back on Quinn, her eyes flew open wide, only now realizing she was sprawled across him, and pushed herself up and off him. "I'm so sorry."

"Are you okay?" Aunt Eileen and Sally May had come running across the street from the pub and were now hovering over them.

"I'm fine." Eloise stood upright, brushing non-existent dirt from her arms and torso. "Wish I could say the same for my peaches and tomatoes."

Sally May was already gathering the wayward produce and putting it back in the bag. "It's not all ruined. Most of them are barely dirty."

"Are you planning on spending the rest of the day napping on the ground?" Hiding a smile, his aunt did her best to sound stern.

"No, ma'am." Quinn stood up and noticed that despite the two of them landing on the feed sack, it had not split open. Thank heaven or that would have been much more time consuming to clean up than the errant produce.

"I'd say you two deserve a good lunch. Put all this mess in your respective vehicles and come on over to the pub for a hot meal."

Sally May handed Eloise a bag of tomatoes. "Finn's making Reuben sandwiches." She pressed her fingertips to her lips and kissed them before bursting her fingers open wide. "To. Die. For."

"Good idea." He glanced at Eloise. "You have time?"

All she did was nod before bending over to retrieve the scattered purchases.

"Okay, then." Aunt Eileen kissed him on the cheek and turning on her heel, she and her friend of a million years sauntered across the street.

Kneeling down to help her pick up the last remnants of her morning shopping trip into a bag, he smiled at her. "Are you okay? You didn't hurt anything?"

Shaking her head, her mouth teased into a smile. "I had a softer landing than you."

"Glad to have been of help."

That made her smile widen into a full-fledged amused grin. "You hurt anything?"

"Just my pride." It was a miracle that more people weren't mulling about to see him embarrass himself falling, literally, all over a woman.

"Well," she glanced around, "weren't we the graceful ones?"

"I'd rate it a solid eight out of ten." His hands at his side, he continued to smile. "Extra points for aerial herbs."

"Sorry about that." Shifting the rescued bag of tomatoes to the other arm, she pulled the keys from her purse.

"Let me." He took the keys and unlocked the driver-side door, then leaned over and picked up the other bags, placing them in the back seat of the quad cab.

"Thank you."

"You're welcome." How was that for stellar conversation. "I'll put the feed in my truck and meet you at the pub."

Her head bobbed, she closed the car door, then locking it, turned to cross the street.

Why was it he could watch that woman do anything for hours?

"Full house. Aces high." Sally May fanned her cards on the table and grinned at her friends. "Looks like Quinn and Eloise changed my luck."

"Hmm," Eileen grunted. If her nephew and the new chef in town were going to change anyone's luck, you'd think it would be their hostess and not a family friend.

Sally May scooped up her chips and piled them in front of her.

The music playing overhead had Eileen tapping her fingers. By the next verse, she was humming softly to herself. Light from the open door filtered into the family pub. She didn't need to turn around, she knew it had to be Quinn and Eloise.

"I'm in." Ruth Ann tossed her chip into the pot and stared at the hand she'd been dealt, doing an awful job of hiding her smile.

Even though the chips didn't represent real money, the intensity with which they all bet, anyone would think they were playing for cold, hard cash. Tossing her own ante into the pot, Eileen shifted to get a better look at her nephew and house guest. Ever since Gray had taken a liking to Eloise, Eileen had wondered who would be the one to fall for the pretty chef. Carefully watching him walk her to a table, Eileen was pretty sure she had her answer.

CHAPTER TEN

The dark wood interior of O'Faredeigh's felt welcoming after the bright sunlight outside. Music drifted from hidden speakers, something jazzy and familiar that had Eloise tempted to tap her toes.

"Be with you in a minute," Jamie called from behind the bar. "Take any seat you want."

"Best table in the house." Quinn pulled out a chair halfway between the bar and the table where his aunt and friends were playing cards. "Unless you'd rather sit at the bar?"

"This is perfect." Eloise settled into the offered chair, enjoying the peace and quiet. The subtle decorations on the wall, the dark rich paneling, and the dim lights succeeded in somehow making her feel as if she'd been transported far away to Ireland. The pub held that perfect mix of old and new—worn wood floors, vintage photos on the walls, but spotless tables and gleaming brass fixtures. She hadn't realized how hungry she was until the aroma of corned beef reached their table.

Jamie approached, set two glasses of water on the table, and smiled at Eloise. "Welcome to O'Faredeigh's."

"Thank you."

"Here for lunch or just some refreshment?"

"Lunch," Quinn said.

"The usual?"

"Yep. Corned beef and cabbage with a thick slab of soda bread and extra butter." The man smiled wider than the Rio Grande.

"You are a creature of habit." Jamie turned his head. "And for our new chef?"

"I hear that your special today is outstanding."

"The Reuben?"

She nodded, anxious to see if the sandwich was as good as Sally May claimed.

"Good choice." Jamie returned the smile.

"Are the chips really homemade?"

"Sliced thin for crispiness by yours truly every morning."

"Excellent. Please add your house-made chips."

"Will do." Jamie took their drink orders and with a promise of speedy service, headed for the kitchen.

Once Jamie had disappeared into the kitchen, Eloise turned her attention to her lunch partner. "Jamie's smile reminds me of your uncle Sean."

"The Farraday genes run strong. Even though Uncle Sean and Uncle Brian are first cousins, we all are clearly cut from the same mold."

"I can see. But I have a question."

"Shoot." Quinn fiddled with a fork on the table.

"If the family name is Farraday, why is the pub called O'Faredeigh's?"

"Ah. When the first O'Faredeigh came to the United States, the port shortened it."

"I'd heard that happened a lot."

"You'd be amazed. I went to college with a kid whose last name was Calabria, turns out that their ancestor didn't speak English and he wound up with where he was born as his last name."

"Yep," she nodded, "they did the same with one of my grandmothers. Her Irish last name was Noughton, but it was anglicized to Norton."

Sally May's triumphant laugh carried from the card table, followed by good-natured groans from her fellow players. The afternoon sun slanted through the pub's windows, catching the brass rails and making them gleam.

"Do they play cards here often?"

"Usually they play twice a week at the café, but sometimes they'll play elsewhere as the mood moves them."

Squinting at the table, Eloise tipped her head, studying the table. "What are they playing?"

"Poker."

Eloise almost spit out her sip of water. "I'm sorry. Did you say poker?"

Chuckling, Quinn laughed. "Don't let those sweet faces fool you. They're card sharks."

"I thought you were going to say something like canasta, or bridge, but poker?

"Didn't anyone ever teach you not to judge a book by its cover?"

"Apparently not." Shifting in her seat, she glanced over at the card table. Knowing they were playing poker put a whole new spin on things. How many more surprises did this town and this family have in store for her?

The music overhead shifted to a familiar Sinatra tune. From the card table, Aunt Eileen's humming grew louder, her voice adding depth to the melody.

"Is that your aunt I hear?"

Quinn paused to listen, then nodded. "Sounds like it."

"She's good."

"Better than good. Before she moved here to help Uncle Sean raise the family after Aunt Helen died, Aunt Eileen used to be a jazz singer."

"Wow." She paused to listen and wished his aunt hadn't stopped singing and returned to humming.

Jamie arrived with their lunch the rich smell of toasted rye and sauerkraut making her mouth water. A basket of crispy house-made chips accompanied her order. "Can I get you anything else?"

"This looks perfect," Eloise assured him, already reaching for her sandwich.

"Very well. Whistle if you need anything."

Quinn reached for his cousin's arm. "What do you say we turn on the microphone?"

One eyebrow shot higher than the other on Jamie's face. "You realize what will happen?"

"I do." Quinn tipped his head in Eloise's direction. "Our guest wanted to hear Aunt Eileen sing."

"Whatever the customer wants." Jamie spun about and walked toward what Eloise realized was an empty space saved for use as a stage, and he pulled out a microphone stand and fiddle with some nearby equipment.

Whispers could be heard from the card table at the same time the handful of patrons in the pub began pointing at Jamie.

The music shifted from Old Blue Eyes to something different—if she wasn't mistaken, an old Burt Bacharach tune, though she couldn't quite put her finger on it from the opening notes. Anxious to taste the sandwich, Eloise took her first bite. Heaven. Tender corned beef, sharp Swiss cheese, the tang of Russian dressing perfectly balanced. "Oh my gosh."

Lifting his chin toward the stage, Quinn smiled. "That's nothing. Here comes the real show stopper."

As soon as Quinn recognized the song "Say a Little Prayer," he knew his aunt wouldn't be able to resist picking up the mic. Keeping an eye on her table, he recognized the head bobbing and shaking for what he'd seen so many times before. When his aunt and Dorothy and Sally May stood, he knew the real show was about to begin.

Eloise's gaze followed the direction he'd pointed and then suddenly, her eyes sparkled and she turned to him. "Oh, I love this song. Did you ever see the movie *My Best Friend's Wedding*? The scene with this song was one of the best. That and the finale when her friend tells her, 'by God, there'll be dancing.'"

"You like to dance?"

Her head bobbed, but before she could say anything, his aunt tapped the microphone.

Hearing the mic was on, without skipping a beat, Aunt Eileen launched into the second verse of one of her favorite songs, her rich voice filling the pub. Dorothy and Sally May provided backup, reminding him of the Supremes, or any other girl band of the sixties.

The chattering of the patrons eased into silence as everyone inched closer to the stage, all ears on his aunt.

"She's good," Eloise said.

The song came to an end and immediately, Aunt Eileen launched into "Always Something There to Remind Me."

Someone must have texted that Aunt Eileen was singing because the pub door kept opening and folks began to pour in, settling in empty tables around the makeshift stage. Even Finn stopped wiping glasses to watch.

"I take it back, she's not good, she's amazing," Eloise whispered, her sandwich forgotten. "I had no idea."

For spur of the moment, his aunt was putting on quite the show. She didn't do it often, but when she could be talked into performing, everyone walked away happy. Aunt Eileen had done several songs, and then paused, stared at Quinn a moment before announcing, "This is my last song as I have a hot deck of cards waiting for me."

The scattered patrons chuckled. The Tuckers Bluff Ladies Afternoon Social Club was well known in town.

"I certainly hope somebody gets up to dance. I hate it when a good slow dance song is wasted."

Again, folks began chuckling softly. Several notes played. No one moved. His aunt sighed and began crooning—did women croon?—"The Way You Look Tonight." Still no one moved, and then it hit him, that was another song from the movie Eloise had mentioned. Not the last song, but from the movie nonetheless. Pushing to his feet, he offered his hand. "We can't disappoint Aunt Eileen."

Her fingers slipped into his, warm and sure. As he led her to the makeshift dance floor, he couldn't help noticing how perfectly she fit against him.

"I should warn you," she said as they started moving to the music, "I learned to dance in Chicago clubs."

"And I learned at barn raising parties." He spun her gently. "We'll make it work."

Her smile could have powered the whole town. "Yes, we will."

Slowly, another couple joined them, and then one more. The small space became crowded with dancing couples, though it didn't matter, his attention stayed on Eloise. He spun her out, then curled her back into the hold of his arms. She moved with such natural grace. Her eyes sparkled with so much contentment, he wanted to keep twirling her in and out as long as it made her happy.

"You're a very good dancer. I don't believe for a minute that you learned to dance anywhere near a barn."

"Don't let the location fool you. Most everyone in these parts knows how to dance at least a little." To make his point, he spun her out again, pulling her back in a move that had her laughing in surprise. They fell into an easy pattern, part swing, part two-step, creating their own style as they went. He wished the dance didn't have to end.

The music slowed to a stop, and his aunt's voice resounded through the room. "I know I said that would be my last song, but I've had a special request for just one more."

Knowing another song was coming, no one left the floor. Like everyone else, he and Eloise kept their gazes on his aunt. The notes began to play and he immediately recognized her signature song—"At Last." Aunt Eileen pulled the mic off the stand, waved her friends off the stage, winked at Quinn, and began singing.

Every single word seemed to reverberate through him. Holding Eloise close against him, feeling the warmth of her breath against his shoulder, wishing he could pull her even closer and keep dancing for the rest of their lives, he didn't understand what was going on, but he did know one thing, Eloise Carey was the best thing that had happened to him in a very long time.

CHAPTER ELEVEN

All Eloise could hear in the back of her mind most of the last few days was the line from that movie: *By God there'll be dancing*. She couldn't remember the last time she'd been out dancing, or had as much fun—especially in the middle of the day! As a result, for the last couple of days, she'd done nothing but hum "The Way You Look Tonight" and dance around while cooking and readying for the grand opening.

With the group of Red Hat ladies staying at the Parlor B&B, the timing of the grand opening would be the perfect opportunity for drawing in crowds. All of which would be filmed for airing on national television. That happening kept her torn between absolute delight and borderline panic. Closing the oven door, she shook away the negative thoughts, hummed a little more, and reminded herself today was going to be a very good day.

For what had to be the hundredth time today, she checked her phone. She'd been tracking Danny's flight since long before it was ready to take off. Despite leaving thirty minutes late, it was scheduled to arrive any minute now, at least fifteen minutes early. She couldn't remember the last time she was so excited; she had very high hopes for Danny here in Texas.

She'd already changed his bed sheets twice, rearranging the pillows, opening windows to let in fresh air, then closing them again when it felt too chilly. The room across from hers had similar vistas of the expansive lands around the ranch house—nothing blocking their views like a big city—perfect for someone who needed space to breathe.

Her phone buzzed. A text from Danny: *Just hit the*

runway. Will let you know when I find my bag and the drive—though honestly Sis, some guy in a suit holding a sign with my name just feels weird.

Fingers moving rapidly, she replied. *Wait till you see the rest of Texas.*

That bad?

That different.

Aunt Eileen appeared in the doorway. "Any word?"

"Just landed." Eloise wiped flour from her hands on a dish towel. With Aunt Eileen's blessings, she'd taken over the kitchen to make Danny's favorite foods for family dinner: seafood bisque, prime rib with her twice baked cheesy potatoes, and green bean casserole. Real casserole, not the stuff from cans. "He should be here in a few hours."

"We all may die of anticipation before he gets here. Whatever you're baking is killing me."

"When did I die and go to heaven?" Wiping his heels on the boot cleaner, Quinn looked up.

Eloise couldn't help but smile. Whenever anyone appreciated her cooking, it always made her happy. Coming from Quinn it made her very happy. "I was just about to tell your aunt that one oven has Danny's favorite dessert, old-fashioned apple pie, the other has my own variation of cheddar baked biscuits."

Another text: *Driver says there's a town called Muleshoe. Who names these places?*

She did her best to muffle the burst of laughter that erupted at her brother's text. After the time she'd spent in Tuckers Bluff and Sadieville, deep down she just knew, moving here was going to be as good for Danny as it had been for her.

Gray padded into the kitchen, his tail swishing against her leg. There were several things she was going to miss when her and Danny's apartment in Sadieville was ready. Gray was only one of them. "You are the sweetest boy." Scratching under his chin, the dog's tail seemed to pick up speed.

"You better be careful, or Gray may never let you leave." Quinn smiled down at the dog, but there was an unexpected sadness in the cowboy's eyes that left her wondering what had happened. And just like that, the sadness slipped away as Quinn bent over to scratch the scruff of the dog's neck. Maybe she'd imagined the momentary sadness.

"Is Danny going to be willing to share you with Gray?" Quinn teased.

"Of course, he loves dogs. Just hard to do in the city." Danny had always acclimated best to foster homes that had pets; she was hopeful at some point, she and Danny would be able to get a pet of their own once they settled into their own place. For now, Gray and his mate would have to do. Her phone buzzed again.

"Another town update?" Aunt Eileen turned on the oven light, peeking inside.

"No, this time he's asking if Texas has anything besides dust and cattle."

That had the entire room laughing.

"Not likely," Quinn added.

"Do sunsets to die for count?" Aunt Eileen turned off the oven light and surveyed the kitchen. "I will never understand how you can cook such deliciously elaborate meals, and yet the kitchen doesn't look like a bomb exploded."

"There's a good reason for that." She salted the beef. "The health department frowns on unkempt kitchens."

"Good thing too." Quinn's uncle came through the back door. "I've seen some horrors on those live television shows about chefs and restaurants."

"You'd be amazed at some of the kitchens I've had to work in. Needless to say, I rarely stayed long. A clean and well-organized kitchen is key to success."

"And that's what Sadieville is going to have when you open." Quinn winked at her.

"I hope so." She smiled, turning the roast to reach the other side.

Her phone dinged again with another message. *Is everything here so far away?*

Again, her brother's comments made her laugh. Maybe

she should have prepared him a little better for what a change this was going to be. They weren't in the big city anymore. Far from it.

There were a few things Quinn Farraday was sure of. One, he could watch Eloise in her element all day long, any day of the week. The other, he was going to miss having her around. A lot.

Heading upstairs to shower and change from a long day working the ranch with his uncle and cousins, his aunt grabbed his sleeve in the hall. "I didn't want Eloise to hear me."

Quinn nodded.

"I'm concerned about having too many people here for dinner. Hannah says depending on how bad the PTSD is that the whole family could overwhelm him."

From what he'd heard about Danny, and what Hannah had explained to him as well, he'd been worried about the same thing.

"Should I send out the all hands on deck, or leave things as they are with only those of us near the ranch?"

He shook his head. "I have never known your instincts to be anything but spot on. Let's keep it simple. At least for tonight."

"What about all that food?" His aunt looked truly torn.

"Woman, have you never seen your men eat?"

A burst of laughter had his aunt slapping her hand over her own mouth and looking over her shoulder to make sure she hadn't been heard. "You're right. What was I thinking?"

Having showered in record time, Quinn changed his clothes and headed back downstairs. The smell of Eloise's cooking had only intensified. Hannah and her husband had arrived, along with Connor and Catherine, and Finn and Joanna. The women had settled at the kitchen counter and the men were in the living room.

Quinn had rarely given much thought to the social

tendency of women to wind up in one room of a house and the men at another, but right now he really wanted to be in the kitchen with the women—or at least with Eloise.

The sound of tires on gravel had Eloise snapping her head up and practically bouncing with excitement. Quinn followed her to the front door, hanging back as she flew down the porch steps toward the parked SUV.

A tall man unfolded from the back seat. Despite the physical resemblance to his sister, Danny's bearing spoke of military training. But the smile that broke across his face at the sight of his sister was pure joy.

"El!" He caught her in a bear hug that lifted her off her feet.

Quinn watched as Eloise's already sunny nature somehow brightened even more. The siblings' obvious bond made his chest tight. Suddenly, he was filled with the need to do all he could to help Danny adjust, and thrive. He would want to do that for any veteran, but right now, he especially wanted it for Eloise. To always see that glimmer of sheer joy in her eyes.

Danny set his sister down, taking in the ranch house. "So this is Texas?"

"This is just the beginning." Eloise looped her arm through his. "Wait till you see what I've been cooking for you."

"Thank heaven, I'm starved. The snacks on the airplane leave much to be desired." Danny's shoulders visibly relaxed as Eloise led him toward the house. His gaze swept the open landscape, lingering on the distant slopes. "We are definitely not in Chicago anymore."

Aunt Eileen appeared beside Quinn, linking her hand in the crook of his arm. "There you have two very happy siblings."

"Yeah." He couldn't take his eyes off Eloise. "Having her brother here means everything to her."

The siblings reached the porch, Eloise making introductions. Danny's handshake was firm but not challenging, his manner reserved but polite. Gray padded over to investigate, and Quinn noticed how Danny's attention immediately focused on the dog. Gray slowly sniffed their guest the way he had done with Eloise at their first encounter. Only this time, instead of plastering himself against the visiting human the way Gray had done with Eloise, the dog lay down on the ground and submissively rolled over, belly and paws up.

A mirrored image of shock appeared on every family member's face.

"Hey there, boy." Danny crouched, gently rubbing the proffered belly. The dog's tail swished merrily.

"Well, that's new." Staring, Aunt Eileen fisted her hands on her hips.

Uncle Sean came up behind his wife, hands on her shoulders. "Has he ever done that before?"

Multiple family members on the porch shook their heads from side to side as if choreographed.

"That's Gray," Quinn said softly.

"Nice to meet you, Gray." Danny gave the dog one last belly rub and pushed to his feet.

To everyone's surprise, rather than follow them inside, the dog bounded around to the back of the house.

"Well, that was interesting," Uncle Sean muttered.

With a brief nod of her head, Aunt Eileen took hold of her husband's hand. "Might as well all go inside. Eloise has been cooking up a storm, and we're all anxious to get to know you better."

"Over food," Connor added.

Connor's wife chuckled. "You'd think we never fed the man."

That made Danny laugh and Quinn noticed the hint of apprehension he'd detected in his stance seemed to fade away.

Inside, the home beamed with a warm welcome. Everyone alert to the newcomer's comfort.

"Coffee?" Aunt Eileen offered. "Or would you prefer something cold after your drive?"

"Coffee would be great, ma'am." Danny's military courtesy showed through.

"If you're okay with it, call me Aunt Eileen. Everyone does."

"Yes, ma—Aunt Eileen."

"There you go." His aunt beamed.

To everyone's delight, since they were all aware of Danny's challenges, everyone was thrilled that he didn't seem overwhelmed by the size of the family. Of course, when the entire clan came around and descended on him, that might be a whole different story.

Eloise had already started pulling dishes from the warming oven, and the aroma of home cooking filled the air.

"Need any help?" Danny asked his sister. One eyebrow higher than the other, she shot her brother a knowing glare. Taking a step back, Danny raised his hands in a surrender motion and smiled. "Scratch that. What was I thinking?"

The stern expression was replaced quickly with a bright smile and sunny disposition that Quinn had become so used to. It was just one of the many things he loved about Eloise—no matter what, she always had a warm smile... *Loved.* Did he just say he loved Eloise? Of course he did, he loved a lot of people. Even the Sisters. But Eloise? What he felt for her was nothing like his affection for the Sisters.

"Are you going to stand there all night growing roots, or are you going to help get this feast on the table?" Aunt Eileen shoved a large bowl of warm cheddar biscuits at him.

Wrapping his arms around the bowl, he glanced at Eloise, merrily stirring something on the stove, then back to his aunt. "Anything else I can take?"

"Start here." His aunt waved at the doorway to the dining room.

The evening slid by without a hitch, carefully orchestrated by Aunt Eileen to be welcoming without overwhelming. Too bad his aunt couldn't do anything for the thoughts now swirling around in his head. There was no doubt that he loved Eloise's cooking, and that smile, it was infectious, able to lift any man out of a bad mood. Then there was that vulnerability in her gaze that made him want to scoop her up and protect her from the world. And he'd never felt anything like that about the Sisters. So, what exactly did he feel for Eloise?

CHAPTER TWELVE

"**R**eady for the grand tour?" Eloise welcomed her brother, who had caught a ride to Sadieville with one of the production crew. Practically ready to burst at the seams, she couldn't contain her excitement at sharing her latest venture with her big brother.

The morning sun streamed through the front windows, highlighting the rich tones of the restored hardwood floors and turning the brass fixtures to gold. Danny's footsteps echoed in the quiet space as he took it all in.

"This hall is mostly tables, more casual. Eventually, there will be room for dancing if we have live music. The next hall over is a bit more formal, private, and thanks to the carpeting, quiet. Eventually, we hope it will be reservation only."

"This is incredible, El." He ran his hand along the paneled wall to one side, then looked up at the ceiling and the crystal fixtures. "When you said historic building, I pictured something…" He gestured vaguely.

"More rundown?" She grinned. "You should have seen it before. The Farradays are miracle workers."

The cobalt blue drapes she and the designer had agreed on brought a burst of bright to the otherwise classic décor of white table clothes and the carpeting in the next room. One of the tables was already set with gold rimmed white china, and flower vase center table. "No napkins?" Danny teased.

"Depends." She loved that this restaurant would be casual at lunch, and then, by dinner time, convert to fine dining. "There will be white and black napkins depending on what the customer is wearing."

"Excuse me?" He blinked. "You're coordinating

napkins with clothing."

Her head bobbed. "Yes. You don't want a woman in a black velvet skirt to have flecks of white linen on her lap."

"Ah," Danny's confusion converted to a broad smile, "and if she's wearing white—"

"Or pastel."

"Or pastel," he repeated, "then the white linen so they don't have residue of black flecks."

"Exactly." She loved that he seemed as pleased by the detail as she was.

His gaze scanned each of the old photographs of Sadieville's glory days, carefully restored and framed, lining the walls, before landing on the two couples seated at two tables in the quieter room of the restaurant. "I thought you said the restaurant isn't open until Friday?"

"It isn't." For the better part of the week, Eloise had been working with the night servers. While she hadn't been cooking a full menu, Molly had been gracious enough to share her daily leftovers to use for training. The crews had been taking turns being guinea pigs with the servers. "That's a training meal and, if you'll excuse me one moment, I need to address something. Be right back."

She left her brother looking at the photographs while she approached her most recent hire. "Carl, I know you're not used to it, but it's very important that you remember, serve from the customers left and remove the plates from the right. You just served Valerie from her right."

The poor guy looked crest fallen. "Sorry, Chef."

"I know. This is why we're practicing."

"Yes, ma'am."

There were so many things for waiters to learn about the caliber of restaurant she hoped to create when there were no fine dining restaurants within 100 miles of Sadieville or Tuckers Bluff, but she had faith the crop of help she'd hired were up to the task.

"Trouble in paradise?" Danny turned to face her.

"Not at all. And you're right. This is the closest thing to paradise I've ever seen." She linked her arm with Danny's. "Follow me and I'll show you my favorite part."

The double doors swung open to reveal her pride and joy—gleaming stainless steel and state-of-the-art equipment arranged exactly to her specifications.

Danny whistled. "Sweet." Above them, the sound of hammering carried through the ceiling. "What's that?"

"The crew has begun working on our apartment." She pointed upward. "Barring any surprises, should be ready in about six weeks."

"Our apartment?" Danny's eyebrows rose. "Above the restaurant?"

"Perfect commute, right?" She spread her arms, and lifted her gaze to the ceiling a moment. "Though I have to admit, leaving the ranch is going to be harder than I thought."

"They've been good to you."

"They have." Her head tipped slightly as she studied her brother. "Hannah thinks that her equine program could be a good supplement to your other therapy."

"El…" His tone held a warning.

"No pressure." She held her hands out. "But the options there if you want it."

"I'm the big brother, you're not the big sister."

"I know, it's just.." Just what? "If the VA is taking too long to organize your therapy, the equine program could be a good option." They'd both been disappointed to learn that the VA in Midland had transferred his files to Butler Creek and no one in either location seemed to know which end was up. Not that it mattered much, but the fear that he'd slide back to the man in Chicago who couldn't handle the pressures of day-to-day living, tugged at her gut.

All Danny did was nod. Not a word. She had no idea if that was good or bad, but hoped she hadn't taken too much for granted with this move for Danny. She so wanted the best for him.

"So, when do I get to see this easy commuter apartment?" Danny changed the subject.

"Now." Rubbing her hands together enthusiastically, she almost squealed with excitement. Last time she'd been upstairs, demolition was mostly complete and the place was a mere shell. With all the final touches on the dining rooms and training the staff, she had little time to snoop. Besides, the one time she'd finished before Quinn and tried to peek, they'd shooed her away. Though she shouldn't have been surprised, wasn't the final reveal the big event on reality renovation shows? She just hoped they let her in today.

As they headed toward the stairs, Eloise couldn't help thinking how right everything felt. Her restaurant almost ready, her brother here, Quinn making her and Danny's apartment perfect for them. Except for the little snag with the delay in therapy, everything was perfect, Quinn was perfect. If she was going to be honest with herself, it wasn't the ranch, or the views, or the family dinners she was going to miss, it was time with Quinn. And what the heck was she supposed to do about that?

Between the hum of power tools and the thwacking noise of hammers swinging, for a brief moment of synchronized silence, footsteps on the wooden steps alerted Quinn to Danny and Eloise's arrival. He'd been watching the clock for the last hour, knowing that this was the first time she'd seen the apartment since they'd demolished the awkward footprint of the original dwelling from the last century.

Without sheetrock, it might be difficult for her to imagine what was coming. Not everyone could understand the maze of two-by-fours filling a home in the framing stages. They hadn't even gotten to installing the plumbing yet, but he was hopeful that she would be pleased nonetheless.

The door eased open and Quinn set his drill down and approached the two guests. "Watch your step. Some of the floor boards are up so we can run the plumbing."

"Yes, sir." Danny answered first. Eloise merely nodded, glancing down at the gaps in the floor before stepping over the threshold.

Once they were inside the doorway, Quinn hollered at

the crew. "Okay, folks. Take a lunch break."

His brothers and a few of their crew set their tools to one side and in a single file made their way out the door and down the stairs.

Turning to face Eloise, he gestured at the skeleton of rooms around them. "Welcome to your future home, at least the bones of it."

Eye's wide, Eloise inched into the main open space. Scanning from left to right, the corners of her mouth slowly tipped upward as if she were indeed seeing the finished product.

"At this stage it's hard to imagine, but—"

Shaking her head, she cut Quinn off. "No, I can see." Her fingers traced at the bottom frame of what would be the new kitchen windows. Not the original one, but three larger, consecutive windows.

"So you'll have more natural light at the counter," he offered.

Her brother following more cautiously behind her studied the exposed beams overhead. "Original timber?"

"The ceiling, yes. The idea is to leave some exposed for atmosphere. We tried to reuse as many of the original two-by-fours as possible for the walls as well."

Danny stopped at an awkward line of angled wooden supports. Without saying a word, he turned to Quinn.

"Since we removed the supporting wall there, we're waiting on a new beam."

"Look, Danny." Eloise crossed into one of the two bedrooms and stared out the window. "You can see all the way to New Jersey from here," she teased.

Danny nodded, but didn't speak.

"Hollywood bath will be here." Quinn pointed to the open space between bedrooms.

"Hollywood?" Eloise's forehead crinkled in confusion.

"There isn't really enough room for two full baths, so you'll have a sink and toilet adjoining one room, a shared tub shower combo and a linen closet in between, then a sink and toilet on the other side next to the second bedroom."

Head tipped to the side, and one eye closed, she studied

the studs and shook her head. "I think I'm going to have to wait for some more work to be done to see that."

Quinn chuckled. "Trust me. It will be perfect."

She nodded, murmuring, "Always." Her cheeks pinkened slightly as her gaze pulled away from him and turned to face the soon-to-be bathroom again.

"All I have to say is you'd better not be taking any hour-long baths." Danny's tone was light, but Quinn caught the way his eyes seemed to track the distance from the bedrooms to the front door. A good military man is always prepared, but Quinn couldn't help but wonder if maybe Danny was a little more uneasy than he was letting on.

"To make things easier to visualize," Quinn pointed to a kitchen wall, "I took the liberty of taping off where cabinets will be in the kitchen."

Her hands clasped in front of her, Eloise practically shook with excitement. "It's so big!"

"We can't put a professional chef in a kitchen suitable for a mobile home." Quinn moved to stand beside her in the framed-out space. "I know how important counter space is to all cooks. There will be commercial grade everything, just scaled for home use."

He'd spent hours with Neil going over the plans, making sure she'd have everything she could possibly need or want. The island would be big enough for prep work but positioned so she wouldn't feel isolated from the living area. It took a few attempts, but they finally worked the space to include a walk-in pantry.

Frowning, she looked from ceiling to floor at the studs and suddenly her face lit up. "Is this…"

"A pantry." He bit back a smile and nodded.

Her bright smile and soft squeal did something to his chest that had nothing to do with construction dust. He forced himself to step back, to remember this was about making a home for both siblings and not about his growing feelings for her.

Delighted with her enthusiasm, he leaned against the wall and crossed his ankles, watching her practically sail through the room, showing her brother where they'd put the sofa, two chairs, then change her mind and move them closer to the window. When she teetered on which wall would she put the Hoosier, he had to bite back a smile. Wouldn't she be surprised when she learned he was refinishing the old piece?

Her enthusiasm was contagious. The more she carried on about the apartment and the furnishing, the moments of hesitancy and reservation he'd seen in Danny seemed to evaporate, until her brother's smile bloomed in earnest and even grew.

The downside of all this enthusiasm—in just a few weeks, the apartment would be ready, the furniture would be delivered, and they'd leave the ranch. For good. All he could think about was how empty the ranch would feel without her there.

CHAPTER THIRTEEN

Sundays were Eloise's favorite day of the week. Today, while the rest of the family went to church, she stayed home to fix a special treat for Sunday supper. Danny seemed on edge for the first time since arriving a few days ago at the idea of going into town for church. Bless Aunt Eileen, she seemed to sense that was too much for him and suggested Danny might want a little more time to acclimate before going into town and he should stay home. He'd stayed in his room for a bit, but then, with his trusty new friend at his heels, went outside for a bit of fresh air.

The back door slammed shut and she thought it might be her brother, only Quinn came in stomping his feet.

She didn't know enough about ranching, but from the amused glint in his aunt's eyes when he told her why he needed to skip church as well this morning, Eloise hoped the real reason had something to do with her. It was silly, and a little school girlish, but she couldn't help how she was feeling.

Eloise looked up as Quinn stepped into the kitchen, the back door closing behind him. The rich aroma of her meat sauce simmering on the back burner hung in the air. "You're just in time." She reached for the canvas apron hanging by the pantry. "I'm making pasta from scratch for supper."

Silently, Quinn eyed the orderly chaos spread across the kitchen counters—flour, eggs, olive oil, and salt arranged neatly beside her wooden board and rolling pin.

"From scratch?" He hung his hat on the peg by the door. "I thought that's what stores were for."

"Blasphemy." She laughed and tossed him the spare

apron. "Nothing compares to homemade. I've been wanting to try Aunt Eileen's pasta roller since I spotted it tucked away in the pantry."

Quinn chuckled, hesitantly taking the apron. "Glad someone knows what that thing is for. I'm not sure even Aunt Eileen does."

"Now you'll both know." She measured flour onto the wooden board, creating a small mountain. "I'm guessing you've never made pasta before?"

He shook his head. "Can't say it was on my list of life skills to acquire."

"Well, today's your lucky day." She made a well in the center of the flour mound, almost like a volcano. "Hand me those eggs?"

Quinn passed them to her, watching curiously as she cracked four eggs into the center of her flour crater.

"Now for the magic." She drizzled olive oil and sprinkled salt over the eggs. "See how the flour creates a wall to keep the eggs contained? That's the first trick."

"Does it always work?" He leaned closer, genuinely interested.

"Not always." She smiled, remembering countless messes in culinary school. "Which is why we start in the center and work our way out. Here, I'll show you."

Using a fork, she began beating the eggs, gradually incorporating flour from the inner walls of her volcano. Quinn watched, his eyes gleaming with focus and teetering with fascination at the transformation as the mixture slowly became more solid.

"This is where it gets hands-on." She set the fork aside. "Ready to get messy?"

His brows shot up a moment before he stretched out his arms and rolled his sleeves up, revealing tanned forearms. "I'm all yours."

Now her brows rose to her hairline and then she had to hold back her laughter when he realized how those three little words could mean something totally different.

"Uh," he cleared his throat and swallowed hard, "I mean, uh," He sighed. "Never mind."

Chuckling, she returned her attention to the mound in front of her. "Start pulling in more flour, like this." She worked her fingers to incorporate more flour into the sticky mixture. "Don't worry about getting it perfect. Pasta dough is forgiving."

Quinn's large hands looked almost comical next to her practiced ones, but he followed her lead, cautiously working flour into the developing dough.

"That's it," she encouraged. "Now we need to knead it until it's smooth and elastic."

Quinn's expression remained skeptical as they worked the dough together. "How do you know when it's ready?"

"I feel it." She pressed her palm into the increasingly smooth mixture. "It'll tell you when it's right. Here, try."

Placing her hands on either side of his, she guided them to the dough, surprised by how naturally he took to the motion—pushing forward with his palms, folding the dough back, turning it slightly, and repeating. The kitchen filled with comfortable silence, broken only by the soft sounds of kneading and the occasional gust of wind rattling the old windows.

"You're a natural," she observed, ignoring the urge to place her hands on his again as he worked the dough.

"Had a good teacher." His voice came out softer than usual, almost intimate in the quiet kitchen.

The dough gradually transformed under their hands, becoming silky and elastic. When Eloise pressed her finger into it, the dough sprang back immediately. "Perfect." She brushed flour from her hands. "Now we let it rest."

"Rest?" Quinn's eyebrows buckled together. "Dough needs a nap?"

Wrapping the dough in plastic, she didn't bother to hide her laughter. "Thirty minutes, minimum. Gives the gluten time to relax. Otherwise, your pasta fights back when you try to roll it."

His eyes crinkled at the corners. "Can't have rebellious pasta."

"While we wait," she grabbed a cutting board, "we can prep the sauce. Hand me those mushrooms?"

They fell into an easy rhythm—Quinn chopping where directed, Eloise stirring and seasoning. She found herself increasingly aware of his movements, the careful precision he brought to each task. The same attention to detail he showed in his construction work translated surprisingly well to cooking, expertly mincing garlic as she'd shown him. She tossed the additional ingredients into the simmering sauce and stirred. Taking a small taste, she seemed content with the seasoning.

"How long does the sauce have to cook?"

"Hours."

"Hours?" Those eyes popped open wide again.

"Here." She held her hand under a spoon and drew closer to his mouth. "Taste."

He blew softly before slurping up the taste of red sauce. For a second she thought, his eyes were going to roll back in his head. "Whatever you're doing, keep it up. This is the best sauce I've ever had."

"And it's not done yet either."

The timer dinged, signaling the dough had rested long enough. Reluctantly, Eloise took a step in retreat. Too bad she didn't have the nerve to move forward instead of back and kiss the drop of sauce away from the corner of his mouth. Now wouldn't that be something worth keeping up?

Eloise turned to clear the counter, dusting it liberally with flour. "Ready for the tricky part?"

What he was ready for was to toss the pasta aside, pull her into his arms and kiss her senseless, but that was sadly out of the question. "Ready as I'll ever be."

She unwrapped the dough, cutting it into manageable sections. With her palm, she pressed on the first piece. Hands much smaller than his moved with a confidence that spoke of years of practice. The same hands that had made that incredible sauce now worked magic with flour and eggs.

"You really love the kitchen." It wasn't really a question.

Continuing to mix the ingredients in front of her, she nodded. "One of my foster parents was a pretty good cook. Learned from her Italian grandmother. That's where I learned how to make the spaghetti sauce, or gravy as she called it. She's the one who taught me to use carrots instead of sugar to cut the acid of the tomatoes."

"Having tasted the sauce—er, gravy—so far, I'm really glad she shared her secrets."

A shadow fell over her eyes. "We were only with her for a couple of years when she had a stroke. Couldn't take care of us anymore, so we moved to yet another foster home."

"I'm sorry." He didn't know what else to say. Right about now, he wished that she'd had a happy and loving family to live with all her life. She hadn't said much, but he knew most of the homes were less than optimal. He was terribly tempted to pull her into a hug and promise her that her life would be forever perfect.

On a deep sigh, she reached for more flour, spreading some on the counter, and placing a drop on the tip of his nose. "Oops."

"Oops?" He let out a laugh, about to reach for the open flour container.

"Ah, ah." She shook her head, giggling and shoved a dish rag in his hand. "We have pasta to make."

"Mm," he muttered, wiping the flour from his nose. "Pasta."

"That's right. Pasta." Still giggling under her breath, she picked up a rolling pin. "First we need to flatten it. Starting in the center, you work outward."

"You, as in me?"

Her grin widened, but she didn't say a word. Just in case she was planning another flour attack, he took a half step in retreat.

He tried to concentrate on the dough rather than the sweet smile that always seemed to have a way of making his stomach do back flips whenever she flashed it in his direction, or the way the sunlight shining through the kitchen windows caught the golden highlights in her hair.

"Your turn." She handed him the rolling pin.

His first attempt was too heavy-handed. The dough stuck to the wooden surface.

"More flour." She reached across him to add flour.

"Careful with that," he teased.

Holding a scoop of flour in her palm, she teasingly held up her hand as if about to pelt him with the whole shebang. Chuckling softly, she merely waved her hand, lightly dusting the counter.

Her shoulder brushed his, heat shot through him all the way to his toes, his fingers tightened on the rolling pin and he sucked in a deep breath.

Oblivious to the sensations running through him, she continued as if they hadn't been teasing each other. "And a lighter touch. Like you're coaxing it, not forcing it." Her voice was soft and low and just as tantalizing as the brief brush of shoulders.

Making another effort, surprise caught him when the dough began to yield under his gentler pressure. "How about that? It's actually working."

"Of course it is." Her smile got him every time. "You build things. This is just another kind of building."

Loving how she looked at life, he rolled the dough thinner, watching it transform into a translucent sheet.

"Perfect." Her approval warmed him more than it should. "Now for the fun part."

"I thought we were already having fun?"

"I thought so too." Still smiling, she turned and fed the dough through Aunt Eileen's pasta machine. "Another trick, don't rush this either. Turn the crank very slowly." The sheet emerged even thinner, more delicate. "You try."

Their fingers brushed as she passed him the dough. He focused on the task, afraid she might read in his eyes what he barely understood himself.

The kitchen fell quiet except for the rhythmic turning of the crank.

"Now we cut." She changed the attachment on the

machine. "Fettuccine or spaghetti?"

"Chef's choice." He'd never felt like smiling so often in his life.

"Fettuccine." She nodded firmly. "Holds the sauce better."

Together they fed the sheets through again, this time watching them emerge as perfect ribbons of pasta. She gathered them, creating little nests on a flour-dusted tray.

"That's it?" he asked. "We're done?"

"For now." She covered the pasta with a clean towel. "They need to dry a bit before cooking."

Her hands were flecked with flour, a smudge of it on her cheek. Without thinking, he reached out, his thumb brushing it away. "Flour." His voice came out rougher than he'd intended.

"Thanks." She didn't step back.

The air between them seemed to thicken. *Say something*, he urged himself. *Anything. Tell her how you feel.* "Eloise, I—"

The back door swung open, the patter of paws spilled into the kitchen seconds before Danny's laugh, shattering the moment.

"Perfect timing." Eloise stepped back, her smile a little shaky. "Quinn and I just finished making pasta."

Danny's eyebrows rose as he surveyed the flour-dusted kitchen. "Looks more like a mess is what you made."

Quinn forced a laugh, though everything in him wanted to grab those lost seconds back. What had he been about to say? What would she have answered?

Another moment and the front door creaked open, the sound of laughter and chatter drifting through the home as the kitchen filled with family. Quinn found himself watching her interact with the different members of his vast family as if she'd always been one of them, debating whether or not he'd imagined the disappointment in her eyes when they'd been interrupted. Wondering if he'd ever find the courage—or the moment—to finish what he'd started to say.

CHAPTER FOURTEEN

"Are we ready for tonight?" Eileen flipped the grilled cheese sandwiches. Everyone was walking around just a tad anxious about tonight's grand opening.

"What would happen if I said no?" Eloise looked a surprising shade of pea green.

"You're not nervous, are you?"

Doing her best to grin as wide as she could, Eloise shook her head before shifting to a nod. "Scared to death," she laughed.

"Nonsense. We all know how good you are. The whole town is dying to eat at your restaurant."

The poor woman's face changed from wicked green to ashen gray. "That's what I'm afraid of."

"There, there, dear." Eileen turned off the stove top and walked over to where Eloise searched her bag. "All will be well. I promise."

The way the young chef's face lit up, Eileen got the feeling she hadn't heard that very often in her life.

Taking a chance, Eileen pulled her house guest into a warm embrace. "We'll all be there to cheer you on, but you don't really need us. You're a great chef, and a good boss, and tonight will not disappoint."

"Thank you." Eloise's smile reached her eyes this time as she straightened, clasping the truck keys from her purse. "Is Danny outside with Gray again?"

Eileen shook her head. "No. He got a letter in today's mail run, and I don't think he liked it, because Gray came across the room and sat at Danny's side. Now the two are upstairs in his room."

"Oh." Eloise's eyes narrowed. "I didn't hear any noise or I would have knocked on his door."

As if summoned by his sister's will, footsteps tapped down the stairs and across the hardwood floors until he came to a stop in the doorway. "Hey, Sis."

Eileen hadn't known Danny very long at all, but even she could see that smile was as fake as Nancy Bergman's boobs.

"You ready to go?"

He shook his head. "I'm a bit tired. I think I'm going to stick around here. Maybe later see if Sean wants a little help in the barn."

"He always wants help on this ranch," Eileen teased, hoping to induce a little sincerity in that smile. No glory.

"Oh." Eloise seemed to be debating what to say next. Straightening her shoulders, and bobbing her head, she plastered on a forced smile of her own. "That's a great idea. Not much you can do at the restaurant but helping out around here would be nice."

Still holding that same half-hearted grin, Danny nodded. "Yeah. That's what I thought." He waved at the two ladies, and the dog still on his heels, turned and headed back to his room.

Eloise spun about and looked at Eileen. "Who was the letter from?"

Shrugging, Eileen shook her head. "Don't know. I didn't see it. Sorry."

"No, nothing to be sorry about."

"Do you have time for lunch?"

Her hand immediately flew to her stomach. "Couldn't eat a bite. I'll snack at the restaurant once I'm sure everything is on track for tonight."

Though she didn't like sending anyone out on an empty stomach, Eileen understood battling nerves. "Fair enough. Go and knock 'em dead."

Eloise laughed for real. "I sure hope not."

Covering her mouth with her hand, Eileen had to laugh as well. "Break a leg?"

Still laughing, Eloise nodded. "Works for me."

Eileen kept her eyes on Eloise until the door closed behind her. She had no idea what was going on with Danny and that letter, but nothing was going to mess up opening night for that sweet woman—not if Eileen had anything to say about it.

It had taken Eloise a good long while to settle into her role for the day and stop worrying about Danny. The VA had dropped the ball and in the short time since his arrival she could see his confidence slipping. Hannah and others had offered him some time with the horses, but Danny seemed determined to wait for the VA. Maybe she was over-worrying. Everyone was entitled to have an off day, even her brother. Checking her reflection in the restaurant's bathroom mirror one last time, she couldn't help but smile. The pristine white chef's coat with her name embroidered in blue looked perfect against her black pants. Tonight was finally happening—after weeks of preparation, menu testing, and training staff, the restaurant was opening to the public. And according to Aunt Eileen, who she'd learned was never wrong; everything was going to be perfect.

The dining room gleamed. Every table set with crisp white tablecloths, polished silverware, and small vases of wildflowers Sarah, her head server, had arranged that morning. The kitchen hummed with activity—everyone scurried back and forth like ants on a mission.

"Everything good in here?" Eloise asked, stepping into her domain.

"Yes, Chef," they responded in unison, the respect in their voices warming her.

The sound of footsteps on the stairs drew her attention. Quinn appeared in the kitchen doorway, work boots and jeans grimy from the apartment renovation.

"We're finishing up early," he said, washing his hands at the prep sink. "Don't want hammer sounds during your big night."

She smiled, grateful for his thoughtfulness. "How's it looking up there?"

"Plumbing's done, electrical's done, waiting on inspections to close it up." His eyes swept appreciatively over her chef's whites. "You look official."

"Feel official too." She checked her watch. "Forty-five minutes until doors open."

Her staff busy with last-minute details, one in the pantry, another in the walk-in fridge, more in the main dining room, they were momentarily alone in her prized kitchen.

"Nervous?" Quinn seemed to linger by the sink, not ready or willing to leave.

"Maybe I was a bit this morning, but now that I'm here and it's all coming together, excited might be a better word." She blew out a long slow breath. "Though my brother looked like he might pass out when I mentioned how many reservations we had."

Quinn nodded. "It will probably be a while before he's okay with crowds. Maybe never. Not everyone likes crowds."

"I know, he just, well, he didn't used to be that way." She straightened his collar without thinking, then recognition dawning, her hands stilled. "Sorry."

"Don't be." His voice dropped lower, his hand took hold of hers. "I like having you fuss over me." Something in his expression made her breath catch. The kitchen suddenly felt warmer, the space between them charged with possibility.

Neither dared blink. His head dipped slightly, and her mouth went dry as her heart raced like a thoroughbred waiting for the sound of the starting gun and the gate to open. When his lips brushed gently against hers, she was pretty sure that racing heart stopped. A whisper of a kiss, over almost as soon as it began, yet still sent sparks of electricity rushing through her.

The sound of the cold storage door latching shut, and several voices calling out around them, sent them pulling apart. Those beautiful blue eyes had darkened to the color of storm clouds.

"For luck," he murmured.

The rest of the evening passed in a blur of activity. By six-thirty, every table was filled. A slew of Farradays had come, as well as the sisters, and a plethora of Red Hat ladies, Danny conspicuously absent but sending a good luck text that made her smile. The production crew filmed discreetly from strategic corners, capturing the restaurant's debut for the show.

Eloise moved between kitchen and dining room, checking plates, greeting guests, ensuring everything ran smoothly. Whenever she caught Quinn's eye across the room, that moment in the kitchen hovered between them like a shared secret.

Near eight o'clock, she spotted Danny slipping quietly through the front door. He'd come after all, taking a small table in the corner where he could watch without being surrounded. The tension in his shoulders was visible even from across the room.

When she approached his table, he managed a smile. "Looks like a hit, Sis."

"You came." She squeezed his shoulder.

"You can thank Gray and Aunt Eileen for that."

"Excuse me?"

He chuckled, an earnest chuckle. "Aunt Eileen explained that no matter what else is happening in the world, this would be your only opening night, and everything else could wait."

She had a feeling that Quinn's aunt was referring to that unknown letter in her own way.

"And Gray, well, he convinced me that I'm stronger than I think."

"He did, huh?"

Danny nodded.

"Do I want to know how he did that?"

With a shrug, Danny raised his hands. "Would you believe, he told me?"

That made her laugh. "You know, I actually would believe that."

"There you go." Danny lifted the menu to read.

"Whatever you want is on the house."

He bobbed his head at her and holding the menu, looked over the edges at her. "You go do you. I'll be fine."

Oh how she hoped so. At first her brother had seemed so relieved to be in Texas, but things weren't coming together the way she'd imagined. Something was bothering him, she knew it, could feel it in her bones, but didn't have a clue what to do or say about any of it. Was it the lack of therapy, or had moving him here been a mistake? And who was that letter from that seemed to have nudged him into a darker place? Taking a second to give him a fast kiss on the cheek, she spun about and chiding herself for worrying too much, returned to the kitchen, catching Quinn watching her. When their eyes met, his expression softened. She wondered if that kiss still lingered on his lips the same way it had on hers. More than once she'd been tempted to lift her fingers to her mouth and make sure she hadn't dreamt the whole moment. Though if she were honest with herself, except for her concerns over Danny, everything else in her life right now seemed like a dream. What had she done to deserve this place, this man?

The crowds had thinned. To Quinn's amazement, even though the restaurant officially closed at 9 p.m., at 8:55 folks were still coming in to be seated. From the murmurs he'd heard, the restaurant was going to be a huge success. It already was.

From where Quinn sat with his family, he'd noticed Danny slip in quietly and settle in a small corner table. When he'd stood to invite Eloise's brother to join them, his aunt, the mind reader that she seemed to be, grabbed his wrist and shook her head.

If there was one thing he'd learned as a kid and been reminded of as an adult, it was never argue with Aunt Eileen—you will definitely lose. So he'd kept one eye on

Danny, and enjoyed his meal with his family. Now that everyone else at the table had said their good-nights, thanks to the long drive back home and children rising early in the morning and dragging their parents out of bed, maybe now was the time to approach Danny.

A second dessert in one hand and a cup of coffee in the other, he weaved his way to the corner table. "I've been abandoned. Mind if I join you?"

Having kept his back to the Farradays most of the night, Danny glanced over his shoulder and spotted the now empty table. He hesitated a bit longer than Quinn would have liked, but finally nodded. "Sure."

"Thanks. I'd have looked awfully silly all by myself at that big table, and I'd only get in the way if I retreated to the kitchen."

"Everyone seems to be having a good time." Danny fiddled with a dessert spoon.

Quinn nodded and stabbed at his crème brûlée with his own spoon. "Have you tried this?"

"Not here, but I've had El's crème brûlée. It's definitely five stars."

"Six," Quinn deadpanned, delighted to see a twinkle in Danny's eyes that matched the twitch in his smile.

"You like her, don't you?" Danny said.

"Of course I do. Everyone likes your sister."

"That's not what I mean, and you know it." The smile had slipped, but the darkness in his eyes had disappeared. He was in protective big brother mode.

Holding his spoon over the creamy dessert, Quinn heaved a sigh and looked up at Danny. "Yes. I like your sister."

Their gazes level, Danny studied him longer than Quinn liked. "You do know, if you hurt her, I'll see to it there's hell to pay."

"I'm not going to hurt her." The words tumbled out before he even had time to think about it. If anything, he was more worried that she'd give up on Texas, go back to Chicago or some other place more exciting than this corner of the world, and leave his heart shattered in itty-bitty pieces.

Danny suddenly leaned back, his shoulders the most relaxed that they'd been all night, his eyes pensive, serious, and suddenly sparkling. "You love her."

It wasn't a question, but he nodded anyway. Until now, he hadn't wanted to admit that even to himself, but this was no time to be kidding anyone. Not her brother, and not himself. "I've never met anyone like her."

"They say the way to a man's heart is through his stomach." Danny offered his first sincere smile in days.

"Not to be trite, but like the movie said: She had me at hello." He debated whether or not to pry, but everyone had been tiptoeing around Danny for days. "Want to tell me why you sat all by yourself?"

"No."

"Okay." Quinn stabbed at his dessert again, afraid to look up. "You got a problem with me and your sister?"

The silence hung so long that Quinn raised his gaze to meet Danny's. Dark eyes, lacking all light stared at him. Danny was fighting his own private battle and Quinn didn't have a clue what to say or how to help.

"No." Danny heaved a sigh. "I think this is where my sister belongs." His gaze darted around the new restaurant. "Here, in Texas. Here with you."

Something in Danny's tone raised the hackles on Quinn's neck. "And you? Do you belong here?"

His gaze dropping to the dessert again, Danny stared long and hard before blowing out a slow shallow breath. "You know, I think I may have a dessert after all."

Quinn didn't know what demons the man was battling. He wished that he, his family, and Eloise could talk Danny into giving Hannah and the horses a chance to ease whatever troubles seemed to be fighting him. Quinn understood that they needed to be patient, but he couldn't help but think something was bringing Danny down and if he gave up on his sister and this town, it would break Eloise's heart, and Quinn wouldn't be able to handle that. Somehow, he had to find a way to help save Danny from himself. He just had to.

CHAPTER FIFTEEN

Years of waiting tables in college helped Eloise balance two mugs of coffee as she knocked on Danny's door. He'd missed breakfast, and even Gray had abandoned his post at the kitchen door to follow Danny upstairs.

"Come in." Danny sat cross-legged on his bed, one hand absently stroking Gray's head while the other held a letter. She could only assume it was the letter Aunt Eileen had mentioned yesterday. The dog's tail thumped against the quilt in greeting.

"Thought you might need this." She set his coffee on the nightstand, noting the VA seal on the letterhead. "Mind if I join you?"

He waved at the chair by the window. "Just shove the clothes to one side. I need to do laundry anyhow."

Though she would have preferred to gather up all the clothes and take then down and toss them into the washing machine, she was more worried about her brother than his clothes and opted to do as he said. When he didn't say anything, she braved asking a question. "Anything important?"

"Just more bureaucracy." He took a sip of coffee, but his usual morning appreciation of her brewing skills was absent.

"Your therapy?"

"Sort of."

"Sort of?" Was that like a little pregnant? She didn't dare tease, he didn't look in the mood.

"Just some paperwork about my disability rating." He folded the letter carefully. "They do reviews sometimes.

Could explain the hang-up with my therapy here."

"What kind of review?"

"The kind where they decide if you're as broken as you used to be." His attempt at a laugh fell flat. "Apparently, I'm doing better."

"That's good, isn't it?"

"Sure."

"No offense, but that doesn't sound very convincing."

"It could also mean that they'll cut my benefits because clearly I don't need as much support anymore." He took another sip of coffee.

"By support, you mean financial benefits."

He nodded.

Now she understood. Danny didn't like depending on the government for a disability benefit any more than he liked depending on her. The expectation was that some day, hopefully sooner than later, he'd be able to handle the day-to-day stress of holding down a job, but they both knew he wasn't there yet. Not even here.

"Maybe I can get Uncle Sean to teach me how to milk a cow."

His tart remark wasn't a question. "This isn't a dairy farm."

"Well then, I have even more to learn, don't I?" His tone left her more worried than she'd been when she knocked on the door.

She perched on the edge of his bed. "Danny…"

"I guess I could become a ranch hand. Can't be too hard to learn to rope cattle." Though his words held less sarcasm than before, she knew he wasn't being serious.

"Danny."

"Or maybe sheep herding. Gray could teach me."

The dog's tail thumped faster at hearing his name, but Eloise noticed how tightly Danny gripped his coffee mug.

"The Farradays don't have sheep either." She tried matching his light tone.

"Horses then." He fiddled with the edge of the envelope. "Hannah's always talking about her therapy program."

"You've talked to Hannah?"

"About me? No. Just a casual suggestion, more of an invitation." His fingers tangled in Gray's fur. "But I hear things. See things. Like how peaceful everyone looks around the horses."

Something in his voice made her pause. "If the VA isn't coming through for you, maybe you could give Hannah a try?"

"Maybe." But his gaze had drifted to the window, to the endless Texas horizon.

She'd never had the nerve to ask him this, but now seemed as good a time as any. "What did you think you'd want to do? You know, when you're done with therapy."

His shoulders hefted in a casual shrug. "I guess I just thought when I was better, I'd know."

No wonder he seemed so lost. She'd always had her dreams, he'd clearly lost all of his.

"Remember that summer job I had at the bike shop?" His gaze remained fixed on a distant point outside.

The sudden change of subject threw her. "In high school? Before you enlisted?"

"Yeah. Owner was a Vietnam vet. Used to tell me working with your hands was the best therapy." He picked up his coffee again. "Tuckers Bluff doesn't have a bicycle shop."

"Oh, that could be fun."

Danny glanced up at her, offering a weak smile that didn't quite reach his eyes. "Maybe."

"Look how much fun it's been starting the restaurant."

Now his smile seemed more genuine. "You did good, El. It's a hit. I knew you could do it."

"You can too."

"Cook? You're mad." The teasing tone was back and even though she was still worried, she felt herself relax just a bit.

"You can open a bike shop if you want. I can help, the Farradays will support you. It could be fun for you."

His gaze drifted out the window. "Maybe."

He wasn't bouncing with enthusiasm, but looked less

troubled than he had when she'd entered the room. She'd have to talk to Quinn, maybe he would have some ideas. Just the thought of Quinn made her insides warm, but this wasn't about her falling for Quinn, this was about saving Danny. She reached for his empty coffee mug. "Want a refill?"

"Nah. Think I'll take Gray for a walk. Maybe talk to Uncle Sean."

"Yes. That's a good idea." She patted his leg and pushed to her feet, taking a moment to scratch the dog's ears. Leaning over, she whispered into Gray's ear, "Take care of him."

As much as Quinn dreaded the day Eloise would move out of the ranch house, he wanted so badly to make this apartment perfect for her. Wiping sweat from his forehead, he screwed the last cabinet on the kitchen wall and then removed the support two-by-four that kept the cabinets level.

"Looks great." Ryan stood in front of the cabinets. "I wouldn't mind moving into this place myself."

If it meant being with Eloise, Quinn wouldn't mind either, but that was a thought for another day.

"Have you heard from Mom lately?" Ryan slipped his tool belt off and placed it in a nearby bucket with some of his other tools. Every worker on site had their own bucket with their own tools and anyone caught reaching into the wrong bucket would have their head handed to them on a silver platter.

"Nope. Though I did talk to Dad yesterday. He's trying to talk Mom into coming down to see what we've done to the town in person."

"Ha." Ryan rolled his eyes. "I don't think we could get Mom to come to Texas if Jesus Christ himself invited her."

"At least she's stopped whining for us all to hurry up and come home." Quinn glanced around the place. His mom held out hope that when the rehabs were done, the remaining single sons—him and Ryan—would go home and settle down for good in Oklahoma. The way he felt any time Eloise came to mind, his mother was going to have to accept that if she didn't get her behind to Texas, she would have to settle for seeing her sons on a few select holidays a year. Very few.

"Oh, my." Eyes wide, mouth slightly open, and oblivious to the camera crew tracking her perusal of the new apartment, Eloise crossed the threshold into her soon-to-be new apartment.

Ryan's gaze darted from Eloise to Quinn, a sly smile crossing his lips. "I'd better meet up with the crew. I hear Molly has something new on the menu for today."

Quinn nodded, but kept his gaze on Eloise, waiting for the moment she noticed the new addition to the kitchen, besides the upper cabinets.

"Hi, Ryan." Eloise shifted her attention to Quinn's younger brother. "Looks like it's coming along well. Thank you."

Ryan waved his arms outward. "We're all just doing our jobs."

"And you're doing it beautifully—excuse me," she grinned at the two, "*y'all* are doing it beautifully."

Ryan lifted his hand, palm out, and did a high-five with Eloise. "Atta girl. You'll be a full-fledged Texan before you know it."

Unlike the merriment in his brother's demeanor, Quinn found himself grinding his back teeth. Even though he knew Ryan had no interest in Eloise, the fun-loving playful moment didn't sit well with him.

Ryan took a step back. "Sorry I missed the opening last night. I heard the restaurant is a smash."

"We had to turn down reservations for tonight." Her smile bloomed even brighter than it had a moment ago.

"Great." Ryan turned to Quinn, his expression falling. There was no need for words, his brother could read Quinn's dissatisfaction. "Well, I need to meet up with the others or lunch time will be finished before I get to eat."

"Oh," Eloise's gaze shifted to Quinn. "I don't want to keep you. I just wanted to come see how things were going before the rest of the kitchen staff arrives to start prepping for tonight."

"No worries. I was just finishing up. Molly stays open till the crews go home."

"Ok. I'm heading out. Will see you later." Ryan gave a brief wave and took a short step in retreat.

"Oh." Lifting her arm to wave at Ryan, her head stopped mid turn as her gaze fell on the Hoosier. "Oh. My. Heavens." Her head immediately spun around and stopped in Quinn's direction. "You?"

He nodded.

"Yeah, well..." Ryan chuckled. "I'll leave you two alone." Without another word, he'd scurried out the door and trotted down the steps as though someone had set the place on fire.

Slowly, Eloise walked to the space Quinn had etched out for the antique piece of furniture. He held back a smile as her hand slowly brushed over the metal counter space. When she reached under it and easily drew the work shelf out and back in then squealed with joy, Quinn's heart swelled in his chest.

"You like it?"

"Like it?" She spun around and before he knew what hit him, she'd leapt in his direction, threw her arms around his neck. "I love it!"

Unable to resist, before she could step back, he wrapped his arms around her waist. "I'm glad. Very glad."

Her arms still wrapped around his neck, her voice softened. "Thank you."

Struggling to form words, he managed to eek out a gravely, "You're welcome."

He couldn't help himself. Having her pressed up against him, her warm breath against his neck, he dared dip his head to bring his lips to hers. Tentative at first, careful, nervous, he pressed his mouth against hers. When she returned the effort, he pulled her in even closer, putting everything he'd come to feel for her into the kiss. If the world ended right now, he'd die a happy man.

CHAPTER SIXTEEN

Sunday dinners at the ranch had become Eloise's favorite tradition. The weekly family meal was the big family event that every foster child dreamed of. This was also just one of the things she was going to miss about moving out. Today's pot roast filled the house with savory aromas while she, Catherine, and Joanna peeled potatoes at the kitchen table.

Quinn and his brothers carried dishes and silverware into the dining room, but Aunt Eileen had thrown them out of the kitchen whenever they threatened to help with dinner. The working dynamics of this family always made her smile.

"I haven't seen Danny. Is he in the barn with Uncle Sean and Finn?" Catherine glanced over her shoulder.

Eloise shook her head. "He fell asleep in the car on the way home from church. He went upstairs to bed for a short nap."

"He did say something about a headache." Hannah stood by her aunt chopping carrots.

"I think all those people were a bit overwhelming for him." Aunt Eileen dropped her carrots into the massive pot.

"Hasn't the VA assigned him a therapist yet?" Her hands still, Hannah looked over her shoulder.

Shaking her head, Eloise sighed. "No, he reported as told, was given a pile of forms to fill out and then nothing. Meanwhile, instead of becoming more lighthearted, he seems to be slipping away. It didn't help any getting a letter the other day informing him of a status re-evaluation."

Aunt Eileen stopped stirring the pot and looked up. "That doesn't sound good, does it?"

"I don't know. Danny said it's normal, they do that from time to time, but I could tell it has him even more unsettled."

Quinn appeared in the doorway, sleeves rolled up. "Need any help?"

"Nope." Aunt Eileen placed the cover on the pot and turning around, placed her hands on Quinn's back, and gave him a nudge. "Go wait with the rest of the men."

His eyes widened and leveled with Eloise's. With a slight shrug, she smiled at him, delighted when he winked back at her before joining his brothers and cousins.

Outside the kitchen window, a brownish haze seemed to be blowing in.

"It's getting awfully windy out there," Eloise commented casually.

"Yeah." From the sink, Aunt Eileen looked out the window. "Sally May's knees were bothering her yesterday. She says the weathermen have it wrong. The little storm is going to be a doozy."

"Uh-oh." Catherine looked up from her potato. "Sally May's knees are never wrong."

"Is that why Uncle Sean and Finn are in the barn on a Sunday afternoon?"

Aunt Eileen nodded. "Just making sure everything is secure. The radio's calling for high winds by evening."

Hannah gathered potato peelings and dumped them into the trash, while Eloise placed the potatoes in the pot.

"Speaking of secure," Catherine dried her hands on a dish towel, "Connor mentioned something about the horses getting skittish."

"Already?" Hannah's brow furrowed. "Usually they don't act up until the storm's closer."

"You know as well as I do that the horses know before we do." Catherine shrugged. "They've been restless all morning."

"Hmm." Hannah looked outside the window, her eyes narrowing. "I'm starting to agree the weathermen may have underestimated the incoming storm."

Aunt Eileen stood by her niece. "There goes Connor.

I'm guessing he's thinking the same thing you are and going to check on the horses."

The wind had picked up enough to scatter leaves across the yard, the trees swaying with each gust.

Quinn appeared in the doorway again, Ryan and Morgan at his side. "The leaves out front are blowing like a whirlpool. We're heading out to help Uncle Sean fill the troughs and cover the feeders."

In the short time Eloise had been here, there hadn't been any storms. She'd just assumed that the lack of rain was perfectly normal for dry West Texas. It hadn't occurred to her that if a storm did hit, it could be a problem. Though everyone seemed to be taking the whole thing in stride, something felt very different about the casual determination with which everyone was preparing. "Should I be doing something to help?"

"No." Aunt Eileen patted her arm. "Dust storms happen in this part of the country all the time. We're going to let everyone else do their thing to secure the situation, which basically means, make the animals comfortable so the wind and rain doesn't unsettle them, and keep the food sources as free of dust as possible. For now, we'll let this roast simmer to perfection. Then we'll all sit down for a nice dinner."

"How long will the storm last?" She couldn't keep her eyes off the gusts of wind raising the leaves in swirls outside and how the skyline seemed to be darkening faster than earlier in the day.

"Depends." Aunt Eileen shrugged, tossing more potatoes in the pot.

"On what?"

"On if the weathermen are right, or Sally May is."

She had no idea if the woman was serious or teasing, but somehow she felt sure if a tornado came through, as long as she was with the Farradays, all would be well. Lifting her gaze to the ceiling, she wished that feeling extended to Danny. Him, she was still worried about. If only she knew what the VA was up to.

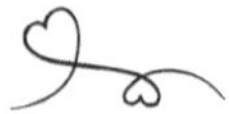

Followed by most of the men in the family, Quinn hurried into the house, brushing dust from his sleeves.

Uncle Sean was the last one inside, securing the door behind him. "Good thing we installed new windows last year."

Aunt Eileen's mouth briefly drew into a thin line. "That bad?"

Her husband nodded. "Temps dropping too fast. Dust is already starting to settle. I'm going to say Sally May's knees are going to be right."

Moving to stand at Eloise's side, Quinn gently brushed her cheek before turning to face the rest of the room. "We've moved most of the vehicles and some of the equipment into the garages, and covered and secured the ones that don't fit."

Uncle Sean nodded. "And the barns and outbuildings are locked and secured, vents closed. Hopefully there'll be minimal dust seepage."

"Good." Aunt Eileen nodded.

For a ranch family, preparing for a little dust up was just another day at work. Quinn just wished things weren't happening so fast. Everything in him said this was going to be a doozy of a duster, and his uncle looked to be thinking the same thing.

"Well." Aunt Eileen slapped her hands together and smiled at everyone in the room. "Dinner is almost ready. I suggest y'all settle down for a bit and I'll whistle when supper is served."

Several heads bobbed as everyone scattered.

Seeing the concern in Eloise's eyes, he reached out and took hold of her hand. "You okay?"

She nodded, her gaze lifting upward to the ceiling. "You guys look like you've got everything under control."

"It's Danny you're worried about?"

"Yeah." She sighed. "He's been napping an awfully long time. I'm torn between checking on him and leaving him be."

"It's okay to check on him." Quinn wished he had some soothing words for her. Truth was he had no clue what was best for a person suffering from PTSD, but he did know that sitting here worrying wasn't good for Eloise. "If you'd like, I'll go with you."

A dim light returned to her eyes, some of the worry—but not all—slipping away. "Thank you."

Taking the hand he held in his and lifting it to his lips, he placed a gentle kiss on her knuckles. "You can always count on me to have your back. Always."

A smile touched the corners of his mouth. Ever so softly, she muttered, "Ditto."

Still holding her hand, he followed her slow pace climbing the stairs. He could feel the tension building in her as she tightened her grip. Halfway down the hall, Danny's door stood slightly ajar.

She tapped lightly. "Danny?" When he didn't answer, she inched the door open.

Looking over her shoulder, he could see what she did. The bed made with military precision, corners crisp enough to bounce a quarter. The clothes that usually littered the chair had vanished.

"Danny?" she repeated, her voice sounding small in the empty room.

Letting go of her hand, Quinn looked into the bathroom. Empty. The counters wiped clean. This was not a good sign. Turning back into the room, he could see the closet door hung open, the hangers empty. No sign of the duffle bag he'd arrived with. On the perfectly centered pillow lay an envelope with Eloise's name neatly printed across the front.

Moving ever so slowly toward the bed, Eloise reached over, her fingers trembling as she picked up the envelope.

Coming up beside her, Quinn placed his hands on her shoulders. If he could think of something appropriate, he would say it, but nothing came to mind. All he could do was stand there and be ready when she needed a shoulder to cry on, because if there was one thing he knew was certain from the condition of the room, she was not going to be happy with whatever the note had to say.

A stronger gust rattled the windows. Outside he could see a dark wall of dust building in the distance. As if punctuating his observations, lights overhead flickered a moment before shining brightly again. Not sure what else to do, he waited for her to open the letter.

Her hands still trembling, she read the letter to herself. Sucking in a deep breath, she closed her eyes and handed Quinn the paper. "He's going back to Chicago."

Quickly, he glanced at what Danny had to say. Basically, he knew the VA would cut his benefits, he knew his sister would have to carry his weight, and he knew that she was falling in love with Quinn and he didn't want to be a fifth wheel. For a short instant, he stumbled over the words falling in love, but brushed them aside. This was no time to linger on how he felt about her or how she felt about him. They had a bigger problem on their hands. If Danny was heading for Chicago, then he was out there somewhere and Quinn would bet his last dollar, Danny had never been in a dust storm and had no idea what he was in for.

CHAPTER SEVENTEEN

"Try calling him. Depending on where the storm is, it might not work, but it's the best place to start." Quinn's words snapped Eloise from her daze.

Her fingers punched one for speed dial. Nothing. The call went straight to voice mail. Whether it was the storm, or knowing she would try to call, he might have turned the phone off, she didn't know. Disconnecting the call, she shook her head at Quinn.

"All right. We need to tell everyone what's going on, starting with Declan."

Of course. In Chicago a person would call 911, in West Texas, you called on the police chief. A plus when the police chief was part of the family. Clutching the letter in her hand, she followed Quinn out of the room and downstairs.

It took Quinn all of thirty seconds to explain the situation.

"I'll call Declan." Aunt Eileen used the land line. In dust storms, cell towers had a way of failing you.

Almost as quickly as Quinn had brought his aunt up to the moment, his aunt had explained everything to Declan. She nodded a few times, then just as quickly wished him Godspeed and hung up. "All right. Declan's radioing Reed to search for Danny en route to Butler Springs. Then he's putting out an APB or whatever it is the police do when searching for a missing person."

The words missing person almost stole Eloise's breath away.

"He's also going to call Adam to check all the places in

Tuckers Bluff Danny might go to, starting with the café and the pub."

"Is driving around town safe for Adam?" Catherine frowned.

Aunt Eileen and Uncle Sean looked at each other, an entire conversation seemed to take place with only their eyes until Eileen nodded and Sean answered, "Safer than walking."

This time Catherine blew out a sigh, bobbed her head and with Connor having come in the back door, she grabbed hold of his hand.

"What about the buses?" Quinn asked. "Any chance he thumbed it to Butler Springs and caught a bus out?"

"I'm sure Declan will reach out to all outlets for Danny to leave."

"All right. I'll start tracing his possible steps from here. If he's still on foot, even in a few hours, he can't get that far in cattle country." Quinn squeezed Eloise's hand before letting go and turning around.

"Hang on." Uncle Sean pulled a map out of a nearby drawer and spread it out on the coffee table. "Once he's off the property, he's got a five-mile walk before he has to choose which direction to go in. Toward Butler Springs— the most likely choice to get to a bus station, the same road into Tuckers Bluff—"

Connor cut his father off, "That is the only route he knows."

"It may be the only road he's traveled since arriving," Ryan faced his cousin, "but Mr. Google could be his travel guide."

"Ryan's right." Uncle Sean tapped at the map. "The third choice is the southern route to the interstate. That's the longest road so my guess is he won't try that."

"He's very upset," Eloise interrupted, her mind rushing back to the times she'd find Danny hiding in a closet or living on the streets. "He may not be thinking rationally."

"In that case," Uncle Sean folded the map, "we won't discard any option."

"Deputy Reed is heading out to Butler Springs, so that

route is covered." Before Uncle Sean could finish his sentence, the kitchen phone rang.

"Yes." Aunt Eileen had to be upset to answer the phone so abruptly. "I see. Of course. No, we won't. I know. Declan James Farraday, your father has been combing this land since before you were a twinkle in your mother's eye… that's better." Heaving a deep sigh, she hung up the handset and turned to her family. "The Brady's truck broke down on the other side of town. Storm's coming from that direction so Reed needs to do an about-face."

Everyone waited in silence for their aunt to divulge more.

When no one said a word, not even their uncle, she sucked in another deep breath. "He said no heroics. If the dust storm is as bad as folks are expecting, well, everyone be careful."

Eloise's heart tightened as if clamped in a vise. She didn't have to be a rancher to realize that every person in this room was willing to risk their own safety to find her brother. A man they barely knew. "I can't ask—"

"You're not asking." Quinn spoke at the same time his aunt and uncle opened their mouths, no doubt to say the same thing.

"Morgan and Ryan," their uncle directed, "you two head for the interstate. If things start to look pretty bad, there are two line shacks that way. Like Declan said, don't play hero, take refuge."

The two siblings nodded and turned, seconds before their aunt stopped them.

Aunt Eileen ran into a room off the kitchen and came out with blankets, flashlights, large bottles of water, and what looked like a pair of walkie-talkies like in the movies. She handed everything off to Morgan, then while the two men stood there, cradling the items she'd given them. She grabbed something else, tying a colorful bandana around each nephew's neck. "It's no longer a matter of *if* the dust blows, but when. You'll need these, and there are three more just in case."

The two brothers nodded again. Ryan taking a second to

kiss his aunt on the cheek before they turned and pretty much trotted out the front door.

The back door blew open. Dale, Hannah's husband, came into the kitchen and with one shoulder, shoved the door closed behind him. "I heard from Declan."

Hannah lifted her head, her eyes smiling warmly at her husband.

"The horses are pretty much going berserk despite all that Connor and I did to keep things as settled and as comfortable as possible under the circumstances. I've tossed several sandbags in the back of the SUV, including emergency and first aid. Which way do I need to go?"

Uncle Sean nodded. "Ryan and Morgan are heading to the interstate. Haven't heard from Adam yet, he's checking if there are any signs of Danny in town."

"Then someone needs to check the road from here to town."

On a heavy sigh, Uncle Sean nodded. "Probably."

"I'm ready," Dale answered quickly.

"Not alone," Aunt Eileen snapped.

"I call shotgun." Connor walked to where his hat and jacket were hung.

Eloise's gaze darted from the head of the Farraday clan to Quinn and back. "What about me?"

"This is not a good night for a city girl to be outdoors." Quinn's uncle had never looked so serious.

Eloise's voice dropped to almost a whisper. "Danny's a city boy."

All Quinn could do was to once again offer his hand to her. It wasn't much, but it was the only way he knew to convey that she could count on him, no matter what.

"I'm going too." Eloise tugged her hand away and turned toward the door.

Quickly, Quinn caught her arm. "No." He hadn't meant for that to come out so harshly. "You're better off staying here in case he calls. I'll go."

"We still need to cover from here to Butler Springs." Uncle Sean threw him a set of keys. "My Suburban has more balanced weight than your truck. A soft wind would blow yours right off the road."

"I'll weight it like Dale."

Uncle Sean just shook his head. "This is no time to be Farraday stubborn. Use my vehicle."

"Yes, sir." Quinn nodded. His uncle was right. His truck wasn't the best option.

Catherine stood up. "There are lots of sand bags next door."

"That's right," Hannah chimed in. "We use them to create barriers for some of the training, but you'll need help if you want to beat this nasty storm."

"She's right." Uncle Sean reached for his jacket. "That wall of dust is moving fast. Could be on us anytime now. When it does arrive, you won't be able to see three feet in front of you."

"Has anyone looked out the window?" Finn lifted his chin toward the back of the house. "We're already running out of time. I'll go with Quinn."

"You'll need water, blankets, bandanas, and extra flashlights. Sean's truck already has a first aid kit, hopefully you won't need it, never mind more than one." Aunt Eileen handed Finn two more walkie-talkies. "When the dust hits, as sure as my name is Eileen Callahan Farraday, those cell towers aren't going to be worth spit. They're on the same frequency as what Adam keeps in his truck and Declan too."

Quinn nodded. "Don't worry. We've got this."

His aunt did her best to flash a confident smile, but at the moment, even she couldn't quite pull it off.

"I'm coming." Eloise glared at Quinn.

"Eloise." Before he could say another word, she crossed her arms and tapped one toe.

Hannah actually had the nerve to giggle under her breath before muttering, "I wouldn't waste my breath, dear Cousin."

Grabbing his hat, Finn shook his head. "Looks like we're all going." He turned to Eloise. "You can ride shotgun if you want."

She nodded, waiting for Aunt Eloise to tie a bandana around her neck.

Hand firmly gripping her elbow, Quinn led Eloise to his uncle's SUV. The wind nearly knocked her off her feet. The lack of birds flying overhead drew home the seriousness of the impending storm. Smart animals had sought shelter long ago.

"We'll find him," Quinn promised, helping her into the cab.

"How far could he get?" Eloise checked her watch.

"Since we have no idea how long he's been gone, could be anywhere from three to twenty miles on foot. If he caught a ride, he could be halfway to Dallas by now."

After pulling into Connor's ranch, Quinn looked to Eloise. "You stay in the cab. Finn and I will toss a few sandbags in the back and we'll be on our way."

"I'm not a delicate flower."

The next thing he knew, she was out of the car and carrying sandbags over just as quickly as he and Finn were. Apparently, in more ways than one, he'd underestimated his chef.

Satisfied with the extra weight in the vehicle, they all climbed back inside and tearing out faster than he should have, Quinn turned the SUV onto the main road. From the rear-view window, he could see a massive brown wall chasing after them, eating up the horizon.

Ahead of him, the truck's headlights caught swirling dust devils growing larger by the minute. They hadn't gone but a few miles when static crackled over the radio.

"Adam here. No sign of him anywhere in town. Most folks are hunkering down, but the word is being spread to keep a lookout for him. I'm driving to the ranch. Out."

Connor came over the radio next. "We're on our way to town now. No sign of him yet. Out."

"I'll let you know if I find him first and you can turn around. Out."

"Ten Four," Connor replied.

A few more miles and another voice—Declan's—cut through. "Got a report from Ned. On his way into town a few hours ago, he spotted someone matching Danny's description walking toward Butler Springs."

Eloise's heart jumped. "That has to be him."

Morgan came over the radio next. "We'll keep driving toward the interstate, just in case it's someone else Ned saw. The guy is pretty old. Out."

Eloise turned to Quinn. "Who else could possibly be out on a night like this?"

"Unfortunately," Finn leaned closer to the front seat to be heard over the howling wind, "most villages have more than one idiot."

If the situation weren't so serious, Quinn would have laughed at his cousin's observation. He just hoped that wherever he was, someone found Danny safe and sound, and soon.

CHAPTER EIGHTEEN

The world shifted from a light haze to a brown blur. Wind howled through every crack in the SUV, carrying stinging particles of dust despite the closed windows and their bandanas. Eloise couldn't see the hood, much less the road ahead. She had no idea how they were creeping forward.

Quinn slowed to a crawl. "Based on my odometer, we should be reaching where Ned thought he saw Danny."

A loud thump hit the fender. Debris? A bird? She couldn't tell in the darkness.

Even though Eloise had no idea why under normal conditions anyone would want to magnify their view of the West Texas dust, right now she was thankful Ryan had binoculars to watch the road ahead. "Better stop. There's something blocking our path," Finn called from the back seat. "I think it might be a fallen tree."

"Great," Quinn mumbled, edging closer until the headlights caught the obstruction. "Is that a...."

"Roof," Finn finished for him. "Wonder where the rest of the shed is."

"Especially since there isn't a homestead anyplace near here." Quinn shook his head. "We have no choice. We'll have to move it. I don't dare go around it, there are a lot of cattle grills on this stretch of road. We could mess up a tire or worse, hit a cow." Quinn reached for his door handle.

"Wait." Eloise grabbed his arm. "You can't go out there alone."

"She's right," Finn reached behind him and grabbed a roll of rope. "We all go. Safety in numbers or we might all be blown to the land of Oz."

Taking a few short moments to unwind the rope, he handed the end to Quinn who quickly knotted it around his waist before doing the same for Eloise.

"You two climb out, then I'll step out and tie it around me."

Quinn nodded.

She was thankful the front seats were captain's chairs or she would have had a hell of a time climbing over the console. The moment they stepped outside, the wind nearly knocked them over. Stinging particles of dust burned what little skin was exposed.

Hanging onto Quinn for dear life, who hung onto the door handle, Eloise said her prayers as Finn quickly tied the rope around himself and shouted for Quinn to move forward.

With the winds blowing sideways with the strength of a bulldozer, they fought their way to the front of the vehicle. The small roof, twisted with other debris, was just big enough to cause a problem.

Positioning themselves around the top section, Quinn shouted over the wind, "On three!"

Even with three of them, they struggled to lift the first section. All Eloise could think was even if they succeeded in clearing the road, what would stop it all from blowing right back in front of them? For the hell of it, she stopped and shouted into the air, "Danny!" Nothing.

"There won't be any hearing in this wind. Let's shout on three. One, two, three."

"Danny!" three voices echoed in the wind. Again, nothing.

"Let's get this thing out of here and get on the road." Quinn turned and gripped the edges again. This time they managed to clear to one side. Fighting the wind, they continued to toss the debris aside.

Just as they cleared the last obstacle, a sudden gust sent Finn stumbling backward.

"Finn!" Eloise screamed, watching a dark blob hurtle through the air straight toward Quinn's cousin.

Clutching his shoulder, Finn went down—hard.

Rushing forward, Eloise could see a dark splotch—blood—seeping between his fingers. It took another minute to see a shard of metal had caught him.

"Get him in the car!" Quinn ordered.

Together they half-carried Finn to the back of the SUV. Inside, overhead light on, Eloise pulled out the first aid kit and said a fast prayer.

"Is anyone near-mile point twenty-two? Out." Quinn stared out the window at the swirling mess. He tried one more time. Hearing only static, he gave up and put the radio down.

"How bad?" She gently fingered around Finn's wound.

"Just a scratch." But Finn's pale face betrayed him.

"We need to pull out the scrap." Quinn was addressing Eloise, but leveled his gaze with Finn.

His face ashen, Finn nodded.

Sucking in a deep breath and blowing it out slowly, Quinn gripped the exposed edge and tugged it out.

Blood gushed, and Eloise pressed gauze against it, putting all her strength into stemming the flow.

Quinn rummaged through a bag and pulled out a shop towel. "They're clean. We can use this to help stop the bleeding."

Nodding, Eloise placed the cloth over the bloody gauze, then taped his shoulder. Needing more pressure, she unrolled an ace bandage and wrapped him as best she could. "I'd better stay back here and keep the pressure on."

Squinting, Quinn froze, staring ahead. "There!" He pointed through the windshield. "Something's moving. Could be Danny."

To Eloise, she couldn't tell if it was her brother, a horse, a scarecrow, or wishful thinking moving ahead.

Quinn was already reaching for his door again.

Eloise caught his hand. "Together," she said. "We go together."

"No. You need to stay with Finn." He quickly untied Eloise and Finn from the rope and leaving a good deal of slack, wrapped it around the driver's seat.

"Be careful," Eloise whispered.

Nodding, he smiled at her. "Always."

It only took a few moments for Quinn's back to completely disappear from view. How did things get so bad so fast? Still pressing on Finn's shoulder, she could see some of his color returning. Not enough to be normal, but enough to tell her the pressure was working.

Glancing up, she tried to see any sign of Quinn or Danny. The brown wall was blinding. The rope pulled tight and she said another silent prayer. *Please God, I cannot lose Danny or Quinn. I just can't.*

Blast. Quinn squinted in the distance. What he had hoped was Danny, was nothing more than the longest and skinniest piece of tumbleweed he'd ever seen. Gripping the rope to return to the car and wishing he'd thought to grab a pair of work gloves, he struggled to put one foot in front of the other. When he finally reached his uncle's SUV and grabbed onto the door handle, the wind caught it just right and for half a second he thought the dang thing was going to blow off its hinges.

Slamming the door hard behind him, he looked into Eloise's soulful eyes, shocked when she threw her arms around him.

"Do not ever do that again."

Before he could utter a word, overhead a loud crack reverberated around them.

Pulling away, Eloise looked up. "What the hell was that?"

Lifting his gaze to the ceiling, Quinn wished the tumbleweed had been Danny and they were all on their way back to the ranch. "If we're lucky, lightening."

"And if we're not?"

"Hell may be about to come crashing down on us."

"Hell?" Poor Eloise looked like she couldn't take any more bad news.

"Sound could be an electrical pole about to snap."

"We can't stay here," Finn ground out. "Either go forward or go back, but we can't stay here."

"Forward." Quinn straightened in his seat and turning the ignition, hit the gas. The car lunged before once again crawling along the dark road at the pace of a sick snail. "Eloise, I want you to tie yourself and Finn to the rope again. If anything happens to… the car and we have to get out in a hurry, I don't want to lose either of you."

"Not me," Finn winced. "I'm not going anywhere. And I'm not sitting up to tie that thing around me."

Quinn hesitated. "Fair enough."

"What about you?"

"I'll tie it if we stop again." Her brows buckled, her mouth hung open no doubt ready to protest when he beat her to the punch line. "I promise, first chance we get to stop somewhere safe, I'll link with you."

With a grunt and a nod, she quickly untied the rope from the seat, attached it to herself, then reattached it to the seat. "Done."

"Good."

As if Mother Nature was laughing at their efforts, a massive crack split the air.

Finn yelled, "Drive!"

Knowing what was coming next, he watched the expression of sheer horror take over Eloise's face as a power pole seemed to dip in slow motion.

Quinn gunned the engine; whether or not they were on the road, the side, or about to tangle with more tumbleweed didn't matter, he had to get Eloise to safety.

Pressing harder on the gas pedal, he kept an eye on the rearview mirror. The falling pole crashed down only inches behind them, then, as if it weighed nothing more than a feather, flew into the air again.

What goes up must come down. If pushing the pedal any closer to the floorboard would make the SUV go faster, he would push his foot right through the floor. Only a few yards down the road, the pole came crashing down once again. The pole's second landing jolted the SUV hard right. Quinn fought the wheel, squinting through the brown haze.

Where the heck was the dang road?

Movement caught his eye. Unless tumbleweed had suddenly grown arms, they just might have found what they'd been looking for—someone waving frantically.

"Danny?" Eloise leaned forward as much as possible without releasing the pressure on Finn's shoulder.

Easing on the brakes, Quinn edged closer. Two figures materialized in the headlights. They were pressed against the back end of a small car. Looking closer, not just the back end, the nose of the car was buried in the ditch and the trunk was at least four feet off the ground. At least he thought it was a ditch. Now he understood why Danny and a young man who looked barely out of his teens were on the road and not taking shelter in the vehicle.

Quinn hit the brakes. The kid with Danny looked terrified.

"Get them in here!" Eloise was already reaching for her door.

"Wait." Quinn grabbed the rope still tied to the seat, but it was too late, Eloise was out the door, the wind nearly taking her off her feet.

Danny rushed forward, the wind pushing him sideways as he fought to walk a straight line. "El, stay put. The road is washed out!"

"What?" she cried back but the voices were muffled in the wind.

The next gust hit like a freight train. Eloise's feet left the ground, the rope pulling taut as she slid sideways. Danny lunged for her but missed.

"Eloise!" Quinn flew out of the seat, hanging onto the rope. For one horrible moment, he couldn't tell if she was still attached. Then he felt her weight, heard her cry out. The rope stretched, threatening to snap.

"I've got her!" Danny's voice carried through the darkness. "Pull!"

Together they drew her back, all three tumbling into the vehicle. The young man Danny had been helping squeezed in behind them.

"When Tim saw the road was washed out and slammed

on his brakes, the car fishtailed off the road."

"That wouldn't have been so bad," the young kid's eyes looked like he'd seen a ghost, "but then the side of the road just seemed to open up. I thought for sure we were going to be swallowed up."

"We got out as fast as we could." Danny spoke mostly to his sister. "But we didn't dare try to actually walk anywhere in this."

"No." Eloise shook her head. "You did the right thing."

"Excuse me," Finn said through clenched teeth. "We can catch up with each other later. Right now, we need to get the hell home. That pole may not be the only one wanting to dance with us."

Quinn threw the SUV in reverse, fighting the wind to turn around. Right about now, he would give anything if Scotty could just beam them up.

CHAPTER NINETEEN

After yesterday's darkness, the sunlight streaming through the curtains was a welcome apology from Mother Nature. From where Eloise sat comfortably perched on the living room sofa, the blue skies and chirping birds were a delight to see. It didn't hurt any that neither Sadieville, nor the restaurant had suffered any damage due to those winds. Somewhere in the back of her mind, she had visions of the entire town having been blown away like Dorothy's farm house in the Wizard of Oz.

"How's it feeling?" Aunt Eileen appeared with a hot cup of coffee and a fresh bag of ice.

"Like I lost a fight with a belt sander." She accepted the mug gratefully, then setting it to one side, gingerly readjusted the fresh ice pack on her leg. The angry scrape beneath it served as proof that yesterday hadn't been some dust-induced nightmare.

"Once it scabs over," Aunt Eileen retrieved the melted bag of ice, "I have a wonderful cream that will help with aching and bruising."

"Thank you." She shifted again, took a sip of the warm brew and winced at how the motion tugged at the minor scrapes on her arm. "Now I understand why motorcycle riders wear leather."

Aunt Eileen tried not to laugh. "Look on the bright side."

Wondering where this was going, Eloise glanced at Quinn's aunt.

"You didn't break any nails."

The two women burst into fits of laughter. That was just the light of humor she needed.

"Looks like I'm missing the party." Arm in a sling, Finn came in holding a cup of coffee and sat in his favorite recliner.

"Don't overdo it." Aunt Eileen walked over to him and ruffled his hair as if he were a little boy.

"Brooks said I'm fine."

"Yes. He also said that you shouldn't overdo it."

"Aunt Eileen," Eloise had to laugh, Finn was whining like a three-year-old, "holding a cup of coffee isn't overdoing it."

"No." She glared at him pointedly. "But it all depends on what you do next."

Finn rolled his eyes. "You sound like my wife."

It showed how much Eileen liked his niece-in-law because her smile spread from side to side.

"Is he giving you a hard time?" Joanna came into the living room, her purse slung over her shoulder, a travel mug in one hand. "I have to go into town for a few hours and I don't trust him to stay home and follow Brooks's instructions, so I'm leaving him with you."

"Smart woman." Aunt Eileen spun to face Finn. "You heard your wife. You let me know if you need anything."

Resigned, Finn nodded. "Yes, ma'am."

Joanna spun around. "I heard you took a nasty tumble yesterday." Her face looked almost as pained as Eloise felt.

"Next dust storm I'm wearing chaps and a pilot's jacket."

That had everyone else in the room laughing.

Joanna's expression softened. "How's Danny doing?"

"Compared to the two of them," Aunt Eileen's eyes held understanding, "he's right as rain, but he's gone for a walk."

Panic had Eloise shooting up in her seat.

"It's okay." Aunt Eileen's expression softened. "Gray's with him, and Quinn's keeping an eye on him from a distance."

Relieved, she sat back again. Even without the storm, she couldn't handle Danny running away again. Visions of Danny sprinting toward her as the wind swept her feet from under her made the hair on her arms stand on edge. His face when they'd finally reached the ranch, exhausted and battered, was different—something had changed in him.

"Tim's parents came for him an hour ago," Aunt Eileen continued. "That boy won't be driving in storms again anytime soon."

Eloise nodded, remembering the teenager's shell-shocked expression as they'd struggled back to the ranch through the darkness. Danny had kept him talking, kept him calm. Something had definitely shifted in her brother.

Taking a deep breath, she winced. Everything ached—muscles she didn't know she had protested the slightest movement. Fighting a dust storm wasn't for sissies.

Movement at the kitchen window caught her eye. Danny and Gray walking slowly back toward the house, Quinn at his side. Quinn. The man had literally risked his life along with the rest of his family to save her brother. She'd known almost since the first day she'd met him that he was special. When he refinished the Hoosier cabinet for her, if she hadn't fallen in love with him before, she certainly had in that moment. But when he disappeared into the dust and she had no idea if he'd be able to make it back to the car, she knew then that no matter what, she didn't want to live even a minute without being part of Quinn Farraday's life.

The three stopped, Danny saying something that made Quinn nod.

Her heart smiled at the sight of Quinn with her brother. Maybe having a big brother figure would be part of the answer. Despite everything, Danny looked steadier, more like his old self. She couldn't decide if she was more relieved or grateful that Danny hadn't reverted to the troubled soul he'd been just a day ago. "He was so scared of being a burden," she said quietly.

Aunt Eileen followed her gaze. "Sometimes a man needs to be reminded of his worth. Finding Tim might have saved more than one life last night."

The back door opened, voices drifting in. Danny's laugh—when was the last time she'd heard that sound?

Whatever happened next, something fundamental had shifted in both of them. Now the question was, what was she going to do about it.

If anyone had told Quinn a few months ago that he would be head over boot heels in love with a woman from Chicago, and about to go into business with her veteran brother, he would have laughed in the person's face. And yet, here he was, desperately wanting to pull Eloise into his arms and keep her there safe and sound until they were too old to walk. And then there was Danny. They'd had a good long walk and an even longer talk.

"From the color and swelling on that leg, I'm thinking it's a good thing the restaurant is closed on Mondays." Quinn glanced at the exposed scrape. "Does it hurt much?"

Eloise shook her head, but he had a feeling it probably stung like the dickens.

"I have some news." Danny was rocking on his toes.

Any minute Quinn expected him to float to the ceiling.

Danny inched closer to his sister. "After you mentioned our conversation about a bike shop, Quinn asked around to see if there's ever been a bike shop in town."

"You did?" Eloise's gaze leveled with his. Her voice was soft and low and did funny things to his insides.

All he could do was nod.

"So," Danny continued, "Burt heard about Quinn's interest."

"Burt?" Eloise's face crumpled with confusion.

"He owns Fred's Hardware store," Aunt Eileen explained, waiting for Danny to continue.

"I'm sorry." Eloise set the ice to one side. "Fred's is owned by a man named Burt?"

Most of the Farradays in the room chuckled. Aunt Eileen just shrugged.

"Anyhow…" Danny looked ready to jump out of his skin if they didn't let him finish. "Burt thought it was a great idea, but since there's nothing available on Main Street any time soon, he offered to give some space at the hardware store for new bikes, and he even has a nearly empty store room that we could use for repairs and restoration."

"Apparently," Quinn stepped in, "restoring vintage bikes is a thing. Burt said that if Danny is any good at it, he could even sell the bikes online."

"Really?" Now Aunt Eileen's face carried the curious expression.

"Doesn't surprise me," Finn interjected. "People sell and ship things of all sizes, all over the country."

"Well, if that's true," Aunt Eileen waved a thumb over her shoulder, "you can start with those two beat up old bikes that have been rusting behind the storage shed since before Grace was born."

Danny's eyes looked like they were about to fall out of their sockets when his head spun around, slack jawed, to face Quinn.

"Told you." Quinn shrugged.

"Told him what?" Eloise's gaze darted from Quinn to her brother.

"That there were two bikes on the property that were older than dirt and just as rusty, and that no one would mind if he restored them."

"That's certainly a start," Finn nodded his approval, "but aren't you going to need working capital for supplies as well as new bikes?"

"I could try for a start-up loan. There are programs for veterans," Danny suggested.

Heads in the room nodded, but waited for more.

"That's where I come in." Quinn patted Danny on the back and her brother's eyes narrowed with confusion. Seemed there were a lot of confused people today. "I think it's a great idea, and if Danny's willing to do all the heavy lifting, I'd be real pleased to be the money man partner."

The only thing that felt better than seeing the shock and excitement on Danny's face at Quinn's offer, was seeing Eloise's head snap around to face him, her eyes filled with what he hoped was love.

"So y'all are in the bicycle business?" Finn looked to the two men.

"Are we?" Quinn looked to Danny.

The young man, barely able to hold his excitement, nodded.

"But there's a condition." To his pleasure, Danny remained calm, his shoulders straight, and his smile hadn't faltered.

This time when Quinn spoke, he stared Danny in the eyes. "There will be no more running away and scaring the life out of your sister."

"I've learned my lesson on that. May have taken Mother Nature and the worst dust storm in half a century, but I get it now."

All he could hope was that the fix would be that simple. Though with Gray sitting nearby, his focus on Danny, Quinn had the feeling that Danny would be getting more support than any one man needed.

Inching to the edge of her seat, Eloise slowly stood upright and leveled her gaze with Quinn's. "May I speak with you a minute? Outside."

Something akin to panic gurgled in his chest. All he could do was nod. Had he done something wrong? Should he have talked to her about it first? Of course he should have. Danny was her brother and he'd overstepped. Dang it.

Following her as she slowly crossed the living room and made her way through the kitchen and out the back door, Quinn prepared himself for the dressing down of a lifetime. "I'm sorry," he said softly.

"What?" She turned around to face him.

"I'm sorry?"

"Sorry?"

He nodded.

"For what?"

He was sorely tempted to say for everything and anything she was unhappy about, but he might as well start with the obvious. "For not talking to you before moving forward on a business for Danny."

"You think that's why I asked to talk to you?"

He bobbed his head, then paused. "Isn't it?"

Slowly, she inched toward him. "No. It's not."

Right about now, Quinn wished he was better at reading women, because he had no idea what her eyes were telling him. When she stopped inches away from him, her gaze leveling with his, her breath blowing softly against him, his heart almost came to a stop. Or maybe it actually had and he was no longer in Texas, but standing in heaven only inches from the woman who mattered most to him in the world.

"Why did you do it?"

"Do it?" Okay, now he not only couldn't read women's eyes, he clearly couldn't understand their speech either.

"Why did you go to all that trouble to help Danny?"

"He's a veteran. Not as lucky as my cousin Ethan who made it through multiple tours and came home with a sound mind. All veterans deserve our respect and if we can, our help. I could help. So I did."

"Is that the only reason?" Her voice came out slow and sweet.

He nodded his head, she raised her brows at him, and then stopped nodding and shook his head just once from side to side. Swallowing hard, he peeled his tongue from the roof of his mouth and croaked out, "Because you love him."

Her head tipped to one side, her gaze bore into him like a laser beam eating away at unknown debris. "Because I love him?"

Briefly closing his eyes and sucking in a fortifying breath, he leveled his gaze with hers and thought in for a penny, in for a pound. "And I love you. So who you love matters to me."

A smile began to tip upward at one corner of her mouth before spreading to the other corner, leaving her smiling brightly at him. Before he could fully process what was happening, her arms went around his neck and she lifted up on her tiptoes. "Then maybe it's a good thing I love you too."

A hinge squeaked and Ryan called out, "Are you two planning... oops." Quickly averting his eyes, Ryan backed into the kitchen and the door slammed shut behind him.

Despite their close proximity and momentarily locking lips, the two giggled before pulling apart, her arms still looped around his neck.

"So," Quinn cleared his throat and left his hands on her hips, "you're not mad at me?"

Smiling again, she shook her head.

"And you really just said you love me?"

Eyes twinkling, she bobbed her head at him.

"Is it too soon to beg you to marry me? If it is, I can probably hold out for an hour or two."

Now they were both chuckling.

Giving her a peck on the nose, he sighed and leaning over, touched his forehead to hers. "As much as I would love to get down on one knee and sincerely ask for that beautiful hand in marriage, there's a lot for Danny to work through and he'll need you. But I do promise you this, as soon as he's well enough to let you go, I'll be down on that one knee in earnest."

"And I'm going to hold you to that promise."

EPILOGUE

"**I** didn't realize how large this place is." Ryan placed the roller back in the painting pan.

Meg grabbed a wet rag and wiped a drip. "I loved living here when I first arrived in Tuckers Bluff."

"Well," Danny looked up from painting the trim, "I don't need a lot of space, but the price was right."

"How was the noise level?" Ryan looked to Meg.

"Why?" Danny stopped painting. "Planning on stealing it out from under me?" Since the VA had dropped the ball on Danny's therapy, after the dust storm incident, Eloise had insisted that he at least try working with Hannah. To everyone's delight, between Hannah and the horses, and working with the bikes, Danny was almost a new man.

Ryan shook his head. He knew a good deal when he had it and living at the ranch was the closest thing to perfect. "Not me."

"Here come Quinn and Eloise." Looking out the window, Meg smiled.

Raising his chin to see over the café curtain, Ryan couldn't help but smile at his brother and Eloise. The two had been walking down the street, holding hands, and grinning at each other as if there wasn't anyone else in the world. Any moment now he expected a cat to cross their path and send them flying. Heck, the two were so busy giving each other goo-goo eyes, a cow could cross in front of them and they wouldn't see it.

"Aren't they cute?" Meg kept her attention on the couple turning the corner toward the stairs that led to the apartment over the café.

"Adorable." Ryan hadn't meant to sound so cynical, but

it was frustrating being the only remaining single Farraday. Not that he begrudged his siblings' happiness with the love of their lives, he just wished more of them still liked going hunting instead of staying home with their wives. That actually made him chuckle under his breath. If his brothers didn't want to stay home with their loves, Ryan would worry about them. Like it or not, he was the lone bachelor hold out; at least he would be once Quinn finally found the nerve to propose.

"Oh, this is looking wonderful." Aunt Eileen and Sally May came through the front door, their arms laden with paper bags and taste bud-tantalizing aromas.

Danny pushed to his feet and set the brush down across the can of paint. "Let me help."

"Nonsense." Sally May slapped at his hands. "I might be older than you, but I'm perfectly capable of holding a bag of Chinese food."

"Chinese food?" Meg's head whipped around. "Since when did you two learn to cook Chinese?"

Aunt Eileen shook her head. "I didn't. Seems Finn's new kitchen helper used to work in Chinatown in San Francisco. Yesterday, the guy brought his lunch to work, and Finn was floored at how good it tasted, so today…"

"We're having Chinese food from an Irish pub." Ryan laughed. "Makes perfect sense."

"What makes perfect sense?" Still holding Quinn's hand, Eloise came into the room, the two dressed in old clothes and ready to work.

His aunt straightened her shoulders and having placed the bags on the counter, hefted her hands onto her hips. "We're having Chinese food for lunch."

"Chinese?" Quinn repeated.

"Don't you start too," their aunt groused.

"No, ma'am," Quinn answered promptly.

Standing behind his brother, Ryan was close enough to hear Eloise whisper in Quinn's ear, "Smart man." And just like that the two were batting eyes and grinning like two kids in a candy store again.

"What's this?" Sally May lifted a sheet from the top of

a pile of something, exposing a bright red lady's bicycle. "Oh my."

Danny's face lit up. "That's a special restoration."

The way Sally May's fingers gently brushed at the handlebars, then down to the spring cushioned saddle before stopping at the chrome fenders, Ryan got the feeling she was reliving a favorite memory.

"It's a 1958 Schwinn Hollywood." Danny beamed, the pride in his work showing.

Sally May nodded. "My daddy gave me a hand-me-down bicycle when I was ten. It was older than me and pretty beat up, but it had a nice new basket on the front and I loved it. Rode all over town and then some."

"It was shipped to me in pieces from Dallas. Took me forever to source the missing parts, but the woman who sent it is restoring it for her mother. Apparently, it was her grandmother's bicycle once upon a time."

Aunt Eileen's eyes widened. "They sent it to you from Dallas?"

"Yes, ma'am."

"That's nothing." Quinn grinned at his business partner. "In the few months since Danny started working out of Fred's, his reputation is growing not only around here, and not just in Texas, but we're getting inquiries for vintage bikes and restoration from all over the country."

Eloise squeezed Quinn's hand. Ryan didn't have to be a mind reader or expert on relationships to see the love pouring from her gaze in Quinn's direction, or the same from him. Those two had to be outdoing all his siblings in the cutesy department. And despite his grumbling about his bachelorhood, he couldn't be happier for them.

"Why is the bike here and not at the hardware store?" Aunt Eileen asked.

"Since it's a private restoration, it's not for sale, and there's just not much room at Fred's for more than what's already displayed."

Several heads bobbed.

"Which," Danny looked at his sister, "brings me to some good news."

Ryan had the distinct feeling by the way Eloise's grip on Quinn's hand tightened and she cast a sideways smile at him that he quickly reciprocated, that they already knew the news.

"Sales are going so well with the bikes that we need more space."

"Always a nice problem to have," Aunt Eileen smiled.

"There's more." Quinn drew everyone's attention before nodding at Danny to go on.

"Mrs. Hallanan has decided to retire," Danny continued.

"Oh." Aunt Eileen looked to Sally May as if saying, *why don't we know that?*

"She's going to close the yarn shop and the landlord says when she's gone, we can have the space."

"That's wonderful," Aunt Eileen cheered louder than anyone.

Sally May slapped her hands together and squealed at the same time Meg pulled him into a congratulatory hug. "And you'll be just across the street from this lovely apartment."

"That's the plan." Danny walked over to Quinn, doing so much better with all the people and attention. "Now that I'm all set, and now that my sister is going to be living all by her little lonesome in that nice apartment you finished for her in Sadieville, maybe you should consider making a few changes in *your* life."

Quinn smacked Danny gently on the back of the head like that character on a TV show. "How to kill the romance."

"Romance?" Aunt Eileen frowned, her gaze darting around the room. "Wait, what am I missing?"

Quinn looked to Eloise. "You might as well show everyone."

Tugging at her shirt front, Eloise pulled a chain out that hung around her neck. Dangling from the thick piece of jewelry, a solitary diamond ring hung. "We've been waiting for the right time to share the news."

The poor woman didn't have a chance to get another word in edgewise. Everyone in the room descended on the two lovebirds. Hugs and congratulations were offered as Aunt Eileen stepped aside to call Uncle Sean and then sent a group text to the entire clan. Apparently, there would be a celebratory dinner at the house tonight. Just the family, then they would spring the news on the rest of the town.

From where Ryan stood, it was clear the painting for the day was finished. Quietly, while everyone else chattered and oohed and aahed over the ring, Ryan collected up the paint rollers and brushes and washed them out in the sink. Soon, footsteps thundered up the stairs and one by one, family members in town appeared, adding to the buzz around the officially engaged couple.

Several things occurred to Ryan. First, his mother was going to have a fit when she found out she'd lost another son to Texas. Next, the producers were going to want to recreate all this excitement for the *Construction Cousins* television show. And lastly, he couldn't help but wonder was he going to turn the corner and stumble onto the love of his life. Shaking his head at his own thoughts, two words came to mind about finding a soul mate—fat chance.

MEET CHRIS

USA TODAY Bestselling Author of dozens of contemporary novels, including the award winning Aloha Series, Chris Keniston lives in suburban Dallas with her husband, two human children, and two canine children. Though she loves her puppies equally, she admits being especially attached to her German Shepherd rescue. After all, even dogs deserve a happily ever after.

More on Chris and all her books can be found at
www.chriskeniston.com

Follow Chris' Monday Blog at her website
ChrisKenistonAuthor

Follow Chris on Facebook at
ChrisKenistonAuthor

Never miss a New Release!
Sign up for News from Chris:
www.chriskeniston.com/newsletter.html

Questions? Comments?
I would love to hear from you! You can reach me at:
chris@chriskeniston.com